FIRE STARTER

Stacey E. Harmon

Copyright © 2024 Stacey E. Harmon

No part of this book may be reproduced in any form or by any electronic or mechanical means, including information storage and retrieval systems, without permission in writing from the publisher, except by a reviewer who may quote brief passages in a review.

ISBN:

DEDICATION

For you, Daddy, and all that might have been.
Rest in peace.

1

"There are always four sides to every story: your side, their side, the truth and what really happened."

Jean Jacques Rousseau

AS I WALKED INTO THE LOBBY OF THE LAW OFFICE FOR TAYLOR AND Taylor, it looked and smelled like money. Not only was there an obscene amount of white Carrera marble on the pristine floors and walls, my eyes went to the Van Gogh painting, "The Starry Night." A copy, of course, but still. A 3,000-gallon aquarium divided the lobby, filled with the most beautiful and exotic fish I'd ever seen. The elevators on the back wall led up to overly decorated offices and conference rooms. To the right was a small reception desk, similar to what one would find in an upscale hotel.

The woman behind it was a tall blond who looked like a model. She gave me a once-over, followed by a smile. "Welcome to Taylor and Taylor. You must be London Devereaux." I had passed my first test.

"Yes. I'm here for a deposition with Alexander and Joey Taylor."

"Of course. Please have a seat. I'll let their assistant know you're here. It may be a few minutes. I believe they're running late with another meeting. Would you care for something to drink while you wait?" I was about to say no when she offered champagne.

"Yes, that would be perfect."

I was hurting inside but, like the lobby, I had to impress as well. My normal attire was much more relaxed than the fashion statement I was attempting to make that day. As the co-owner of Devereaux and Sinclair Insurance Group (DSIG), I go into the field after substantial thefts, fires, and other such claims. But not that day. My visit required me to elevate my game in every way. The highlights in my brown hair—which I had gotten done just before my world was turned upside down—complemented my tanned skin. My red Valentino suit, tan rock-stud four-inch Valentino stilettos, Chanel earrings, and Versace purse screamed power and success, even if I didn't feel it.

As I went to take a seat, Robert Young, our in-house attorney at DSIG, stood up to greet me. He was representing me during my upcoming deposition. It would be the same true crime story I'd already shared with the police, minus a few details. This time my audience wouldn't be friendly, considering Taylor and Taylor represented one of the perpetrators or, as they said, "alleged perpetrators." In addition to reading my statement, they were allowed to depose me before I testified in front of a jury, assuming there was a trial.

"London, you look beautiful!" Robert gave me a bear hug as the receptionist returned with my champagne. I thanked her and took a sip. It was ice cold, just the way I liked it. I could tell she was surprised by Robert's hug, but she didn't say anything as she returned to the safety of her perch. "You look surprisingly good considering everything. You don't have to do this right now. I can delay it, especially after what happened to Remy. I'm so sorry about her, by the way. I know you miss your sister. We all do."

His eyes welled with tears, which made me tear up. After we had both regained our composure, he continued. "The truth is the two of us haven't fully prepared for this depo, London. I don't understand the facts myself."

Robert had a good point. Only a few of us knew the truth. My family and I had decided to share the full story with the rest of the world in our own time. For the moment, "the rest of the world" included Robert.

If I had told him, it would put him in legal jeopardy, and I could never do that. He had been working with us for almost a year now. We met a decade ago while studying at LSU. Robert was a bit of a nerd, but he was always helpful in my study groups. He became my tutor and was willing to coach me whenever I needed it. We lost touch after graduation, then ran into each other in Atlanta. We picked up where we left off in school. I became fast friends with him and his wife, Amy. He was an attorney and licensed to practice in the states where DSIG operated, including my home state of Louisiana. Our primary location was in Georgia, but we also had offices in Louisiana and Tennessee. I was grateful to have him on board.

"Thank you, Robert," I said, noticing he had used a bit of extra product to slick down his usually untamed red hair. "I appreciate it, but I want that animal locked up forever—him and his ringleaders. The sooner I assist with this investigation, the sooner he goes to trial and gets convicted. I'll be glad to expose him as a criminal." I knew I had to keep my emotions in check. Normally, I would talk to Remy, my older sister, who was always able to help me keep it together. I suspected she'd remind me of Paul Laurence Dunbar's quote: "Don't forget to put on the mask that grins and lies." But she's been gone for nearly thirty days. Every day without her made it more difficult to remain objective.

"Robert, you know I've been through enough depositions to hold my own even against the Taylor brothers. I'll stick to the facts. I just need you to block and tackle. To object when they ask about what happened to Remy. I'm not ready to talk about that. Not today. Can you do that for me?"

He looked at me as if I had two heads. "If you think I'm just going to sit by your side and smile like Tara Lipinski and Johnny Weir commentating on a figure-skating competition, you're quite mistaken."

I chuckled at that. Robert was a lot of things, but he wasn't the flamboyant figure skater, Johnny Weir. It was the first time I smiled in a while.

"I'm your legal counsel of record," he continued. "I'll interrupt when a question isn't relevant or, in today's case, about Remy. But you must know you'll be compelled to discuss her circumstances at some point. I'll keep you on track to answer questions as factually and concisely as possible. But you need to do three things: trust me, remember you'll be under oath, and know that once we enter that conference room, everything will be recorded even before the actual recording begins. Now, let's talk strategy while we still have time."

I drank the champagne to steady my nerves while Robert and I reviewed the facts, starting with how claims and underwriting leadership at DSIG had noticed a high number of homeowner fire claims over the past year. In addition to insuring cars, we insured a growing number of residential properties in metro Atlanta and surrounding areas. Statistically, house fire losses were less than 10 percent of our claims. Severe or total losses were significantly less, at 2 percent, but lately, severe fire losses had been creeping up. Something unusual was happening.

"I know many of the origin and cause experts in the state. Almost all of them are skilled at their craft. They can filter through fire debris and find everything from faulty lamp wiring to carelessly thrown cigarette butts," I said. "Most recently, six out of ten total fires came back as suspicious, but the causes were undetermined. Somebody is setting fires, and they know what they're doing."

Robert was about to respond when the receptionist approached us. "Ms. Devereaux and Mr. Young. Thank you for waiting. Attorneys Alexander and Joey Taylor are ready for you. Their assistant, Ana, is coming down to meet you."

Robert and I locked eyes. He nodded ever so slightly as if to say, "Don't worry. I got your back."

2

"If you want peace, prepare for war."
A.J. Darkholme

As we walked past the huge aquarium, I recognized some of the fish as poisonous, which shouldn't have surprised me. The elevator doors behind it opened, and a slim Asian woman—presumably Ana—was waiting for us.

On the way to the twentieth floor, we exchanged pleasantries, during which we learned that the Taylor brothers leased the top two floors.

The doors opened to a wave of dark, plush carpet. We walked past an open area with comfortable-looking seating throughout and offices with clear glass walls where at least two dozen well-coiffed men and women were working with purpose. I'd known Alexander and Joey Taylor for a few years, and I was impressed. As Robert and I took it all in, I sensed the employees were taking us in as well. Although the office was new to me, I could tell it was where the magic happened.

Ana ushered us into a conference room with a striking view of downtown Atlanta. After showing us where the refreshments were—water, coffee, tea, and light snacks but no champagne this time—she left.

It was 2:00 p.m. on a Thursday, and traffic was already picking up. Mesmerized by the carefully choreographed ballet on wheels, it wasn't until I heard a cough that I realized the court reporter was seated with her steno writer at the end of the mahogany table, which could seat twenty people.

"Oh, hello," Robert and I said at the same time. After introducing ourselves, we learned that the stenographer—Sharon McBride—had just finished working on the previous deposition. The firm she worked for specialized in deposition videography and stenography. In addition to the steno writer in front of her, a camera was set up on a tripod on one side of the table. It was arranged so that the person being filmed would sit with their back against the windows. I was grateful, considering I usually avoided sitting with my back to the door. Some called it paranoia. I called it situational awareness. As my father used to say, seeing when and where the bullets are coming from allows a person to duck.

Sharon was new to her company, this being only her second time working with Taylor and Taylor. She was a curvy, brown-skinned woman with box braids that extended to her mid back and appeared to be in her late twenties. There was no wedding ring, and I noticed she took a liking to Robert. He picked up on it too. The fact that she was new to her role was a bonus.

Robert grinned at her like the Cheshire cat. "I'm so glad you're here, Sharon."

I frowned. Had he just picked up a Southern accent? He was from Ohio, for goodness' sake.

"We're all in this together to make sure we have the right people testifying for the right reasons. Don't you think so?"

Enjoying the attention, Sharon nodded and smiled.

"Now, Sharon, do you remember the last witness's name?" Robert asked. "It's important, but I can't seem to recall it." He was careful not to use a pronoun because he had no idea who it was.

"Of course," Sharon replied. "It was the primary detective on the case, Jeff Jefferson."

Jackpot! We had what we needed. Robert thanked his new friend, then turned to look at me, one eyebrow raised.

We both knew Jeff. He was the lead detective and very knowledgeable about the case. My head started to ache. I didn't know if he shared everything or just the parts the police agreed would be available to the public. I had to get out of that conference room and find out. Knowing that information would prevent me from possibly perjuring myself and facing up to five years in jail if convicted.

I jumped up to leave, Jefferson's number already called up on my phone, when a line of attorneys, led by Joey Taylor, marched in and blocked the doorway. They looked so ridiculous, walking in step with one another, that I wondered if they copied it from the office scene in *National Lampoon's Christmas Vacation*.

"It's good to see you, London," Joey said. "You're looking as lovely as ever. Thanks for coming."

I laughed on the inside. He had subpoenaed me.

He seemed like he wanted to shake my hand or, worse, hug me, but I stayed slightly out of reach. The pandemic had changed some social norms, which cut me some slack. The Taylor brothers were intelligent, good-looking men with African and Italian ancestry. Both of them had thick black curly hair that most women would have killed for. Their olive complexions gave off a year-round glow that paired well with their dark brown eyes. Both of them were six feet, two inches tall with athletic physiques. Most people couldn't tell Joey and his twin, Alexander, apart, but I could. It was all about the eyes.

There were four Taylor brothers in total: Giovanni, the oldest and the only married sibling; the twins, Alexander and Joseph; and Matteo, the twenty-something "baby."

Alexander was one minute older than Joey, and he never let him forget it. Joey had joined Alexander in his practice several years earlier. He idolized his twin brother, wanting to be just like Alexander when they were younger. They grew up extremely close, excelled in the same sports, went to the same schools, and dated similar-looking women. The three older brothers were in their late thirties and very intense. Thank goodness Giovanni and Matteo had different careers. Four attorneys in the family would have been two too many.

"Thank you, Joey. It's good to see you too," I said, which was a lie. "Let me introduce you to my attorney, Robert Young. He's our in-office counsel at DSIG."

After they greeted each other, Joey introduced the full line of attorneys who had marched in behind him. They all had varying levels of experience, but most of them were junior attorneys there to witness the Taylor brothers in action. I knew about them from my research and recognized each of them from their photos on the firm's website and LinkedIn profiles. They were an eager group with promising careers. I was glad to see the firm was committed to diversity, with the group featuring people from all over the world. The only person missing was Alexander. That gave me an opening to excuse myself to the ladies' room for that much-needed call with Detective Jefferson. I walked out without looking back, leaving Robert to make do without me.

I tried not to draw attention to myself, which was a ridiculous thought considering I was dripping in Chanel and Valentino, but I was able to sneak away to an empty office a few doors down from the conference room. The phone rang several times before Jefferson picked up.

"London is that you?"

"Yes, I don't have much time," I whispered. "I'm about to give my depo. What do I need to know?"

"Crap!" I'm sorry we didn't connect before. The captain was trying to get me out of it until this morning. I didn't finish until about twenty minutes ago. I'm still close to that building.

"London, you're smart. Answer their questions clearly and concisely. And force them to ask follow-up questions. Tell the truth but stick to the agreement. You can't share what happened to Remy without playing our hand."

That was my plan and why I had Robert to help guide me.

"I will. It won't be a problem," I assured him. "How long were you in there?"

"A little over three hours. I've had longer ones, though. London, one more thing. Be cautious with Alexander Taylor. He's intense and committed to digging in. I know you two have a history. He might ask the same question two different ways and then circle back to it twenty minutes later if he's not satisfied with your answer. He'll grab ahold of your ankle and won't let go. He's known throughout the station as 'Pitbull.'"

That used to make me smile, but not that day. Just one of many reasons to feel anxious. I should have had a shot of tequila earlier instead of champagne. I thanked Jefferson for his advice and then made my way to the ladies' room for real this time.

I stared at my reflection in the mirror, trying to see myself as others saw me. Between working out and tennis, I tried to stay active five days a week. Staying healthy and being fit was important to me. My suit fit perfectly and showed off my curves. My hair was usually in a ponytail, but that day I had loose ringlets on my shoulders. Most people said I looked like my beautiful mother. My ethnicity was African, Jamaican, Irish, and a mix of varying European ancestry, which was not unusual being from New Orleans.

As I looked into my hazel eyes, I wondered why Remy and I had been so eager to help the police do their job. Sure, we were trained investigators, and we ensured our employees at DSIG kept their training current as well. The same was true for our older brother, Luke, who is mostly a silent partner. But none of us were in law enforcement. Had our overreach heightened this madness?

I thought back to the beginning when we identified the irregularities of the total fire losses. We should have waited to see what the police investigation turned up. Instead, we jumped into the fraud investigation like a pair of crime-solving Nancy Drews. But even as I chastised myself, I knew we couldn't have stayed on the sidelines. It wasn't in our blood.

It reminded me of when Remy and I were little. She was only two years older than me. When we played hide-and-seek with friends on the block, Remy and I would pair up, determined to win. It didn't matter how good of a hiding place our friends found; they couldn't stay hidden for long. Our friends would get frustrated because not only were we good at finding them—detectives in training, even back then—we were even better at hiding. They rarely found us, and often we just came out after our friends got tired of looking. Luke, who was two years older than Remy, was impressed. The three of us had always been close, especially so as adults.

I smiled in the mirror at the memory but then pushed those thoughts away. It was not the time for reflection or regret. I texted Luke.

Heading into the storm.

He texted back immediately.

Sis, you are the storm!

I loved my big brother.

When I returned to the conference room, most of the people present were engaged in casual conversation, but I could tell they were eager to begin.

Robert was having an animated exchange with the Taylor brothers. I wondered what it was about, but I didn't get the chance to ask because as soon as Alexander Taylor spotted me, he ended the conversation and headed straight toward me.

"There she is. The woman of the hour," he announced in his deep baritone voice, commanding everyone's attention. For the first time in more than a year, I was face to face with Alexander Taylor—the man I had left standing at the altar.

3

"The trouble is you think you have time."
Buddha

Devereaux and Sinclair Insurance Group was housed in a northern suburb of Atlanta. Inside, Luke Sinclair Devereaux still had his phone in his hand as he paced in his office. Starting the business wasn't nearly the risk for him as it had been for his sisters. He already owned a gym, but his sisters, London and Remy, had taken a chance four years ago by leaving their corporate jobs. They never looked back. In just a few years their financial health improved significantly. They ran a successful operation with over sixty employees in Georgia and steady growth each year in their other two states. The company was situated in a multi-use suburban downtown city center where they benefited from referrals and walk-in traffic. The office environment was designed to project a chic, modern vibe with bold colors, open seating, an exercise room, and a bevy of complementary snacks. Fortunately for employees, gourmet food trucks were parked nearby several times a week.

DSIG's receptionist, Serena McFarland, sat with her laptop, computer monitors, and phone at a large charcoal industrial desk with a glass top. She was stationed up front where the public could walk through branded double glass doors during business hours, which ended at 6:00 p.m. A small conference room and a customer restroom were available in the same area. All DSIG employees were given key fobs for access beyond that area into the rest of the building, including what they referred to as "the floor."

Serena was a tall, thick, dark-skinned woman with a short, cropped haircut. As a former Atlanta police officer, she was a professional, but make no mistake; she could kick some serious butt. Remy and London met her when they took Serena's self-defense class and felt she set the right tone in the reception area. DSIG had great clients, some of whom had become friends. However, some policyholders become upset upon realizing their policy excluded certain losses. Serena's presence helped minimize incidents without the need for a uniformed security guard.

On the floor, the adjusters, underwriters, and licensed sales staff had workspaces with laptops and monitors on unassigned desks since their roles were a hybrid of virtual, on-site, and fieldwork. Leadership and assistants are available with cubicles spread throughout the floor. London and Remy shared a talented executive assistant, Lina Bernard, who was in the same area but had a more private oversized cubicle. Although Luke spent most of his time on his other business ventures, three of the four corner offices belonged to him, London, and Remy, with the fourth serving as a supply room.

Luke was nervous. His sister was about to undergo an

important deposition. Justice was needed for Remy and all of them. The family was emotionally exhausted. Their employees were on edge, and customers had legitimate claims to settle. Worst of all, the police were clueless as to who the mastermind was behind it all. That's partly why London had a plain-clothed police detail waiting for her in the lobby and everywhere she went. Luke had been offered the same detail but declined.

Chet Miller, the man awaiting trial for arson, was dirty for sure. He had set fires, lied to people, and destroyed lives. He deserved to go down for a long time. The problem was, he wasn't talking. Either he was afraid to identify his boss or he didn't know who his boss was. His friend, Johnny Lott, had also been arrested. He was involved in setting his own house on fire, but it was obvious he wasn't part of the bigger picture.

Luke was normally a confident man. He had played football in college but an injury in his junior year prevented him from pursuing an NFL career. He was just over six feet with a square jaw, sandy-brown hair, and hazel eyes, just like London. He took his physicality seriously and was an accomplished trainer to professional athletes. That career was booming, but right now his focus was on his family and this business. They were being targeted in ways he had not anticipated, nor did he fully understand.

He was separated. London had introduced him to his estranged wife, Kelly, when they were in college. She was also a fitness enthusiast. She was relatively tall at five feet seven inches, athletic but thin, blonde, and green-eyed. She was a chiropractor and treated many of his clients. They dated for several years and married four years ago, just after they opened DSIG. Over the past two years, however, they had grown apart. Even after counseling, they couldn't reconnect. They tried working things out, but for Luke, it was more out of what was expected and less out of love. Since he moved out a year ago, they rarely spoke, and when they did, it was about the house or the car or some other impersonal matter. He was mentally preparing for divorce, but that was hard to admit and would have to wait for now.

His brother-in-law and friend, Rod Jaymes, stuck his head in the door. "Hey, man. How are you holding up?" he asked as he came in to give Luke the bro-handshake-hug.

"I'm keeping it together. We're dealing with so much, and on top of it, nobody is excited about London being deposed today, especially by her ex-fiancé. But more importantly, how are you making it? Remy's been gone for four weeks."

They both paused, taking that in for a second. Rod nodded. "It's been tough. I go to sleep thinking I'll wake up to find my wife beside me, but when I open my eyes, she's not there. It's a haunting feeling. I've been trying to bury myself in work."

Although one would never know it from Rod's humble demeanor, he had been honored as a 2022 Food and Wine Best New Chef. He was primarily known for his Louisiana cuisine, which often included influences from Africa, France, India, and Spain. He'd dabbled in other cuisines as well, having been a chef for many years. Rod was barely eligible for the prestigious award. He had just met the requirements of the five-year maximum of overseeing a kitchen when he was selected. For the past few years, Rod had been the head chef for a popular, long-standing restaurant in an upscale part of Atlanta called Buckhead.

As trying as his career had been, owning their own restaurant had been Rod and Remy's dream for some time. The opening of the Sophia was close to becoming a reality. They were finally in a financial position to move forward, but that goal seemed to have crashed and burned.

"It's time for me to get away for a few days and visit my parents in New Orleans," Rod said. "I'll be back sometime next week."

Luke scrutinized Rod's face, trying to understand how difficult things must be for him. He noticed the dark circles beneath his brother-in-law's eyes, his normally unblemished light brown skin was missing something. His dark brown eyes were usually vibrant, but not anymore. His black hair was always perfectly cut due to his public profile. Restaurant guests usually wanted to congratulate the chef on their fantastic and creative meals. Now his hair was getting long, and it was obvious he hadn't been eating much over the past few weeks. His thin frame was slighter than usual.

"When's the last time you saw them?"

"Too long. I was heading their way a few months ago, but work always got in the way. I'm headed out to the airport and just stopped by to let you know. Text me when you hear from London about the deposition. I want more than a conviction for both of those jackasses. I want to bring down everybody who's bankrolling them. They're nobodies at the bottom of a big pyramid."

"We all agree on that," Luke replied. "Chet might be the one in the know. He's only been locked up for a short time. Once he gets a true taste of jail, he'll be ready to talk. But for the next few days don't worry about that. And don't worry about us either. Don't worry about any of it. Take care of yourself, and tell your parents we all say hello. We'll connect when you get back."

As Luke and Rod headed into the reception area, they almost ran over one of the senior DSIG supervisors, Wilson Kent. He was a slight, blond-haired man who couldn't have been more than five feet seven inches and maybe 150 pounds. Since he wasn't usually a customer-facing employee, he was wearing one of his trademark hoodies, all of which had a logo or quote on them. This one said, "If you don't like change, you'll like irrelevance even less." It was summertime, but Wilson always seemed to be cold. He was unusually pale, which suggested he didn't venture out in the Georgia sunshine often. Wilson took his leadership responsibilities seriously and had never met a challenge he couldn't overcome, at least at work. He relished putting in a good ten hours per day. At DSIG he felt important.

"Wilson," Luke said, "I'm glad you're on the floor today. We're relying on you to help run things as normally as possible. We need to continue meeting our service levels. To our customers, it's just another Thursday. They can't lose confidence in us."

"Everything's under control," Wilson assured him.

"Have you met Rod Jaymes?" Luke asked. "Remy's husband."

"It's been some time. It's nice to see you again, Rod," Wilson said. "I didn't have a chance to talk to you at the services. I know I speak for a lot of our employees when I say we loved Remy. She is truly missed. I miss her every day."

Rod, who had a good five inches on Wilson, looked down at him. "Thanks, Wilson. I appreciate that. I know she especially appreciated your loyalty. Don't ever forget that. Now, I have to run and catch a plane, but I hope to see you again." They shook hands. Then Rod and Luke headed out the door.

Wilson watched them as they walked out of the office and onto the sidewalk. He knew he was witnessing a private moment between family members, but he felt justified because, in his mind, he was also part of that family. He had been with DSIG before they opened their doors and was one of the first leaders they selected. He helped them build the startup business. Wilson was involved early on with the adjuster and underwriter interviews. They took his recommendations seriously and hired almost everyone he suggested.

Wilson smiled at Serena as he passed her on his way through the reception area to go back onto the floor. Usually, she intimidated him. She was friendly but serious.

As soon as he reached the floor, he heard the buzz. The employees hadn't expected to see Rod. None of them had seen him since Remy's funeral.

"I wanted to express my sympathy but didn't have the chance," one of them said.

"Don't worry," Wilson said. "I offered condolences from all of us. Rod knows how much we all care. The best way to honor Remy is to continue to do the best job we can."

Right then Wilson made a promise. Well beyond what Luke asked, he would do everything in his power to make sure everyone continued handling claims with the same focus on efficiency and quality as always. He would do that for the customers and for the Devereaux family.

4

"Everything is complicated if no one explains it to you."
Fredrik Backman

"Xander," I said, more to myself than to him. "It's good to see you again." I meant it. I just wished the circumstances were different.

"London, I don't know what to say." He gave me the full body scan. "You take my breath away." He took my hands in his and then hugged me like he needed it, so I let him. I owed him that and probably much more. His face touched mine, his lips close to my ear. I think for a minute he simply enjoyed our familiarity and forgot where we were—in his conference room on the twentieth floor with his partner/twin brother and junior attorneys looking on. He must have also forgotten

I had left him a year earlier. And he had certainly forgotten he had subpoenaed me because I was a critical prosecution witness against his client. But I didn't forget any of it, not for a second, and neither did Joey.

"Um, well, I'm glad everyone is here," Joey said. "Alexander, don't you think we should get started?" He squeezed his brother's shoulder, and Alexander reluctantly let me go.

"Yes, of course," Alexander said. "I believe everyone has met. Please take a seat." He cleared his throat. "Ms. Devereaux and Mr. Young, would you mind sitting by the windows to be videoed?"

"Of course, we'd be happy to," Robert said, eager to assert himself. While everyone was getting seated and setting up their laptops, Robert texted me. "*What the hell was that about? That man is either in love, lust, or hate with you. I can't tell which.*"

"*I forgot to mention we were engaged,*" I texted back. "*It's a long story, but bottom line: I broke it off the night before the wedding. It wasn't pretty.*"

Robert pinched the bridge of his nose before he replied. "*Anything else I need to know? Did you have an affair with one of his brothers? Father . . . sister?*"

That one made me laugh. We received some puzzled looks. I shook it off and put my phone away, resuming my professional demeanor.

And just like that, the deposition began. "Ms. Devereaux, you are here at the law office of Taylor and Taylor and Associates to give a deposition related to any knowledge you may have regarding our client, Chet Miller, and the alleged crimes with which he's been charged," Joey said. "Do you understand that you're under oath, to tell the truth just as you would in a courtroom with a judge and jury?"

"I do," I replied, immediately regretting my choice of words when Alexander looked up from his notes and locked eyes with me.

"And are you aware this deposition is being transcribed,

recorded, and videoed?"

I stole a glance at Robert's friend, Sharon. "I am."

"For the record, Attorneys Alexander Taylor and Joey Taylor will be the only ones asking questions. Several junior attorneys are in the room to observe only. Mr. Young, is that acceptable to you and your client?"

Robert and I had spoken about the possibility of junior attorneys attending, and we were fine with it. I was accustomed to having eyes on me.

"We acknowledge their presence and have no concerns with them remaining in the room," Robert replied. "However, we reserve the right to request their dismissal as we continue with the deposition."

Joey nodded. "Duly noted. If we ask any questions that you don't understand, please advise, and we will repeat or restate them. Ms. Devereaux, do you have any questions before we begin?"

"I do not."

"Mr. Young?"

"No."

"Then I'll turn the proceedings over to Alexander Taylor to begin the questioning."

I looked at Alexander and noticed the warmth I had seen just a few minutes earlier was gone. In its place was a cold, deliberate stare that mimicked his brother's. It reminded me of Detective Jefferson's nickname for him—Pitbull. At that moment, it was hard to tell the brothers apart except by their tailor-made suits. At work, they made a point of dressing differently. But in their off time, they had a habit of wearing clothing without realizing it. I had teased them about it a few times but certainly not that day.

After asking the perfunctory questions regarding my name, position, and so on, Alexander dove right in. "Ms. Devereaux please tell us what led you to believe customers were reporting fraudulent fire losses to Devereaux Sinclair Insurance Group, known as DSIG."

"Several months ago, my assistant, Lina Bernard, pulled data for an underwriting review. We were reviewing homeowner losses, and she discovered fire irregularities."

"Irregularities about what?"

"The severity and frequency of fire losses incurred over the past few months were twice as many as expected over such a short period. Lina shared that data with my leadership team. They agreed this needed to be brought forward for further review."

"Could you or your team simply have underestimated the number of losses that would have been reported in a particular timeframe? Surely, it's not an exact science."

"That's why we hire experienced actuaries," I replied. "Our employees use algorithms, statistics, and other data over several years to predict the frequency and severity of claims over time. It's not an exact science, but it is highly unusual for losses to double in a very short time span without a natural event like a hurricane, tornado, or a wildfire triggering damage to a multitude of properties at once."

"You received more losses than you expected. So what? In case you forgot, you own an insurance company. Customers file claims. You must investigate and either pay or deny them regardless of whether they fit into your time frame."

I had to stop myself from rolling my eyes. "Of course, we investigated," I replied. "That's how we determined six fires were set intentionally. It's also how we know your client was involved in starting them."

I went on to share how it had all unfolded. Lina revealed her findings to our leadership team and then to Remy, Luke, and me. Ten fires appeared to be suspicious in similar ways. All of them had several crime indicators, but they had been assigned to different adjusters in different territories, so the connection hadn't been made yet. Some indicators included having small amounts of personal property left onsite that weren't particularly sentimental. No one was home at the time of the losses even though they all occurred late at night or early in the morning. That along with the fact that all ten policies were in the process of cancellation were huge red flags. Another indicator was that in each case, the smoke detectors and fire alarms weren't working. We've all heard a smoke detector chirp and couldn't take the beeping for long. How could all these property owners have just ignored it?

Remy oversaw the investigation and reassigned the files to our quality investigation team, then asked Wilson to supervise the project. The four of us met to establish the next steps. Remy took the lead right away."

"Wilson," she said, "we want our most experienced adjusters on these losses. Have them advise the customers there are questions to address before any payments can be made. Send each one a letter reserving our rights, indicating we are investigating their claim. Depending on our findings, there may not be any coverage. Let's take recorded statements to gather the facts according to them. In the interim, get the fire department reports, and hire separate origin and cause investigators on each one. We need to see what they discover independently of each other. At first glance, I suspect a few of these are accidental losses, but not all of them are. Our initial goal is to differentiate between the legitimate claims and the potentially fraudulent ones as quickly as possible."

Wilson took copious notes as Remy shared her thoughts. She understood the importance of not making too many assumptions before the investigations were complete and made sure Wilson understood that too. We all thought it was a good plan. She was primarily responsible for the claims side of the business. I was responsible for the underwriting operation, and Luke was more involved in sales. But this was significant and would impact every aspect of the business. We were in this together.

We were siblings and partners, alike and different in many ways. We were all in our thirties. Luke was thirty-four, Remy was thirty-two, and I was the youngest at thirty. Remy was short at five feet even, a good three inches shorter than me.

People thought we looked alike, which I took as a compliment. But while I looked like our mother, she took after our father, including his green eyes and fair skin. She changed her hairstyle and hair color often. At the time, it was a burgundy color and hung to her mid-back. It looked beautiful and spirited, just like Remy. Because her husband, Rod, was a chef, they attended many food events. They were serious foodies, which contributed to her curvy figure. Luke was always on her about working out in his gym.

"So, you had a specific plan of attack to investigate each of the losses," Joey said when I finished. "What happened next?"

I looked over at Alexander and noticed he was absorbed in my story.

"We set up a status meeting with Wilson and Lina a few days later and invited the adjusters who were assigned to these losses. During the report, we determined four of the ten appeared to be legitimate claims that we would honor. Although there were crime indicators, the causes of loss came back as accidental for varying reasons. One client lost a pet in the fire. Another lost a family member. The remaining six were marked as suspicious but undetermined. It was time to advise our in-house counsel, Robert Young, and contact the police."

5

"I stopped waiting for the light at the end of the tunnel and lit that bitch myself!"

Keely Spell

I WENT ON TO EXPLAIN THAT THE MORNING AFTER OUR STATUS MEETING, Luke, Remy, Robert, and I shared what we discovered with Detective Jeff Jefferson at the local police station. Jefferson was a forty-something Midwesterner with a headful of dark hair. I didn't know his ancestry, but he reminded me of the man in the old Brawny paper towel ads. After a significant conversation, he brought in his partner, Detective David Kinser, who was the exact opposite in appearance—an older, balding South Carolina gentleman. He had a Southern accent that put people at ease, and he knew how to read the room, which was crucial to detective work. I liked him right away.

They reviewed the documentation we provided and agreed the six losses were suspicious enough to open a fraud investigation. Before we left, we all agreed DSIG would continue handling the claim investigations, which included on-site inspections to estimate the damages and document what remained of the contents. We would request each of our customers to provide a signed, notarized proof of loss declaring the financial impact and their requests of DSIG. In the interim, the police would begin a criminal investigation. We agreed to maintain check-ins throughout.

Once the four of us left the police station, we had a late breakfast at one of our favorite restaurants, Chapter IV. Remy and I sat next to each other. Robert and Luke were across the table. As soon as we had our coffee, I turned to Remy. "I think we should inspect these losses. I want to get our eyes on these."

Remy shook her head in disagreement. "Our adjusters have already been out to each of the sites at least once. Most are going back to finish their scopes, so I think we're in good shape from that aspect."

"No," I insisted. "I think we should see what we can find ourselves." I was talking myself into the idea as it was coming out of my mouth. "These people are potential criminals and are trying to steal from DSIG—from us! They're making serious offensive moves, so we *must* make big defensive moves and then go on the offense ourselves."

Always the pragmatist, Remy took this in while she sipped her coffee, sweetened with bourbon cream. "You realize the origin and cause investigators have already been out, right? Not to mention Detectives Jefferson and Kinser will likely canvass the neighborhood and do whatever else it takes to solve these cases."

"London, what are you suggesting?" Robert asked.

"Sure the police will investigate," I replied, "but I think we might learn more if we approach the neighbors ourselves.

Let's meet people where they are—without the police—where they feel most comfortable, in their own homes. Maybe we can approach them on the weekend when they're still in their jammies. Have them invite us in for coffee while they spill the tea about the neighbors they don't like. Who knows? We might be able to bust this thing wide open on our own."

"Well, we are trained investigators," Remy said. "At this point we have nothing to lose, and we know how to handle ourselves in the field."

"I don't think that's a good idea," Luke said. "Why do you two need to pound the pavement? Remy just explained how everybody else is doing just that."

"Because it's our business. No one else is going to take it as seriously as we will," I replied. "We have to."

He looked at Robert, and they shook their heads, knowing there was nothing they could say to talk me out of it. So, with that, we had a semblance of a plan. Remy and I would talk to the neighbors to see what we could learn about our customers, whom we suspected were out to defraud us.

After breakfast we talked tactics. It was a simple plan. Remy and I would approach the next-door neighbors on each side and directly across from the houses we had insured. We planned to ask for their help to assist their neighbors by providing any information they had. What did they hear, see, or know about the incident? And what did they know about their neighbors? It was amazing to see how quickly people went from advocates to avengers when a seed of doubt was planted in their minds.

As I was sharing my story, Robert brought me back to the present. "It's been almost two hours. I think my client could use a break." I was surprised to see it was nearly 3:45 p.m.

"Agreed," Alexander said, looking at his Patek Philippe watch. "Let's resume at four o'clock."

I was glad for the break. Robert and I left the conference room and found the office I had snuck into earlier.

"You're doing great," he said. "It seems they're content to

let you tell your story without interruption. I suspect that will change when you share what you and Remy learned about their client."

I nodded. "Speaking of clients, I need to call the office and check on things. Luke has Wilson leading the claims department today. He's good but he gets nervous under pressure. I just want to see how things are going."

Not waiting for Robert to respond, I called Wilson's direct line. As usual, he answered on the second ring. "Hey, Wilson. It's London."

"London, are you out of the deposition already?" I could hear the smile in his voice.

"No, just on a break. I knew you'd be there, so I thought I'd see how you and the crew are doing."

"Everybody's fine. About half of the team are working in the office, and the other half are working virtually. Our service levels are looking good at about ninety-four percent. We're projected to end the day at ninety-seven percent, a good two percent over our end-of-the-day target."

"I wasn't worried, but I'm glad to hear it. How are you managing?" In addition to what had happened to Remy, he was in a serious relationship with someone who wasn't exactly trustworthy, and he was always at the office.

"I'm great. No need to worry about me. I'll be here as long as you need me."

"I know, Wilson. But it's important to enjoy a full life, not just a life at work." I was about to tell him how much I appreciated him when Robert pointed at his watch. It was almost time for us to go back in. "I'm sorry, but I have to go. We're about to resume."

"Okay, London. Thanks for calling. See you tomorrow."

After he hung up, Wilson began to hum an old tune by Sly and the Family Stone: "It's a family affair. It's a family affair . . ." He smiled. In his mind, he and London were as close as siblings. He was her brother by a different mother.

As cliché as it sounded, he was always there when she needed a shoulder to cry on. Luke was a good brother, but Wilson felt it was important that he was available to London, especially after losing Remy. He was happiest at work where he was closest to his "family."

His cell phone rang. He smiled as he picked it up, hoping it was London. Maybe she had forgotten to tell him something. Or perhaps she wanted to share a secret just between the two of them. His smile faded as he looked at the name. It was Marge, his live-in girlfriend, or as his co-workers not-so-secretly referred to her, "Large Marge."

"Wilson!" she said. "What time are you coming home tonight?"

"I'm not sure. We're really busy right now. London is out and—"

"London!" She sounded annoyed. "Have you talked to that woman again about using my construction company? She knows we can do anything and everything for those customers of yours. Do you know how much money that little witch is denying us by not recommending me?"

"Marge," Wilson replied, "have you lost your mind? After everything that's happened, there's no way London can recommend your company. There are too many conflicts of interest. Surely, you understand that!" He shook his head in disbelief. "What should my employees say? Hi, Mr. and Mrs. customer. Do you have a fire or water loss? How about you hire my boss's girlfriend's company? They've only been investigated a few times by the Department of Insurance *and* the police, but they can fix you right up!"

He pictured Marge at home. She was probably having a pre-dinner snack. She was a large woman with short, stringy, brown hair. Unlike his pale skin, she had a tan from working—or rather, observing—outside while her construction employees worked. She was slightly taller than Wilson and outweighed him by at least sixty pounds. He wondered why they were together after two years of misery. If he were honest, he would admit she was a little off-kilter. He wasn't the most masculine man, but he could do better than Marge. Maybe London could set him up with one of her swanky girlfriends.

"Did you hear what I said, Wilson?" Marge asked. "I need the exposure. I don't care what your employees say as long as they say it about me. London relies on you. Her brother does too. The least they can do is throw you a bone by using my company. Other insurance companies work with us. She pretends to appreciate you, but she doesn't. I thought she learned her lesson after the loss of her sister and all those fires that could have taken down the business. What will it take to get her to do the right thing?"

Wilson got an eerie feeling, but he shook it off. He looked at his watch. It was already 4:00 p.m. "Marge, London is a good leader and a better person. I don't have time for this. We can talk when I get home."

"Fine. But if that woman refuses to use my company, then you'll leave hers!"

Over my dead body, Wilson thought as he hung up.

6

"The truth is rarely pure and never simple."
Oscar Wilde

WE GATHERED BACK IN THE CONFERENCE ROOM JUST AFTER 4:00 P.M. More snacks and beverages were waiting for us. As soon as I entered the room, Alexander made his way toward me, but Joey blocked him. I noticed it but I don't think anyone else did. Knowing Joey, I imagine he told his brother to sit down, stay on task, and not embarrass himself. It did make me wonder what Alexander would have said to me, though.

Once everyone was seated, Alexander resumed the deposition, his professionalism intact. "Ms. Deveraux, before the break you indicated that you, your siblings/partners, and your attorney shared information with the police that led them to open a fraud investigation into six suspicious fire losses. All parties agreed your company would continue to investigate the claims, but more specifically, you and your sister, Remy Devereaux, determined the two of you would take on a more integral part of the field investigation. Albeit brief, is that an accurate summary?"

I nodded. "Yes, that's accurate."

"Did you canvass the neighborhoods where the fires took place?"

"Yes. Remy and I did that together."

"Alright. Tell us what happened next. How many neighborhoods did you visit?"

"There were six fires in three different neighborhoods. I guess your guy was getting lazy because he started multiple fires in each one. But we got much of what we needed after visiting the first neighborhood."

He started to smile, then caught himself, his face turning serious again. "Tell us where you went and what you discovered."

"Right away Remy and I agreed that Robert and Luke weren't coming with us. Robert, of course, is our in-house counsel, not a claims employee. But more importantly, we didn't want to shut people down before they began by introducing an attorney." I glanced at Robert, who nodded in agreement. "We thought Luke would be too much of a distraction. Whenever we go out, people ask if he's an athlete. Although we might have been able to use that in our favor, we needed to keep people focused on the fires.

"That Saturday morning, we headed to Dunwoody, a part of town where two of the fires took place. I drove while Remy looked for the first address. It was an older neighborhood. Most of the houses were one-story ranch-style homes made of brick with single-car garages. Even though the houses had been built decades earlier, most of them were well maintained. Several people were out mowing their lawns or working in the gardens when we pulled up.

"If we hadn't seen the pictures and the mailbox with the address on it, we would have driven by the house. It was a simple, thirty-year-old red brick structure. From the street, it appeared to have minor fire and smoke damage, even the front slope of the roof was somewhat intact. But once we got closer, we saw that the entire right and rear elevations were gone, and the interior of the house was completely exposed to the elements. Only the front and left exterior walls were standing. Everything inside was burnt. It was a hot fire that started in the garage, burning everything in its path."

"What did you do once you pulled up to the house?" Alexander asked.

"We had put our DSIG signs on the van before we left, and we wore branded shirts and identification around our necks, so it was evident we were with the insurance company. We got out of the car with our boots and khakis on and walked around the house to see the full scope of damage.

"We rang the doorbell of the neighbors on the left. The front doormat said, 'Welcome—The Carnes.' We were hoping to talk to them first but were disappointed when no one came to the door. It was obvious why they were the first to call 911. Their house was the closest to our client and had large floor-to-ceiling windows facing the front and sides, with some of them looking out toward our customer's home. They would have seen the flames. If the fire department hadn't contained the fire, there was a good chance the Carnes' house would have been damaged as well. I got the feeling the house had stories to tell.

"As we returned to the sidewalk, a slim, older white woman approached and introduced herself as Henrietta Lane, the neighbor on the other side of our client's home. She told us the Carnes had just left for vacation, and they'd be gone for two weeks. I wasn't happy to hear that, but there was nothing we could do about it. Remy and I introduced ourselves and let her know we were trying to finalize the claim. 'It's a darn shame to see such a beautiful home go up in smoke like this,' she said. She told us she knew the original owners, Earl and Dody Lott. They built the house in 1971 and had their son Johnny that same year. 'I'm sure Johnny and his new wife hated to lose a house that was in his family for so many years,' she added.

"'New wife?' Remy asked, seeking to engage her in conversation. 'Oh yeah,' she replied. 'Shelia is Johnny's third wife. He hasn't been lucky in love. The first two didn't last more than five years combined. Hopefully, this one is his forever love.' I asked how long they'd been married and if Johnny had any kids. She told me she couldn't be sure who belonged to which wife, but he had five kids. They visited her sometimes. She said Johnny and Shelia were talking about having a child of their own. He had asked Henrietta to take a picture of them in front of the house with all the kids just a few days before the fire.

"I bet he never imagined this would be the last family picture they would take with the house in that way," she said as she pulled it up on her phone. The photo featured Johnny, who looked to be fifty years old or so with a skinny, but pretty and much younger dark-haired woman. There were five children ranging from a sixteen-year-old girl to a four-year-old boy. The kids all resembled their father, with dark hair and blue eyes.

"Since Henrietta seemed so willing to talk, Remy and I tag-teamed her with more questions. Remy asked where the kids lived now, and Henrietta said mostly with their two mothers. 'What about Johnny's parents?' Remy asked. Henrietta told us that 'Big Earl' passed away a few years ago, but his wife, Dody was living in an assisted living facility a few miles down the highway. However, she was planning to move back home soon. When I asked if Dody was planning to move in with Johnny and Shelia, Henrietta said she was planning on having them move out. She wanted to live in the house she built with her husband, hiring a caretaker to look after the grounds.

"Henrietta Lane proved to be extremely helpful. Although

it was all circumstantial, she provided a treasure trove of information to share with Detectives Jefferson and Kinser. Johnny was our insured's son and seemed to have a few incentives to burn his own house.

"We thanked her for the help and then walked toward the back of the burned-out house. The caution tape was still around that portion of the house. As Remy and I were looking around the property, something caught my eye on the left. Remy noticed it too. No one had answered the door, but someone was home next door at the Carnes' house. We saw them walking past the huge floor-to-ceiling windows. It was difficult to know for sure, but it appeared to be a teenage girl. She hurried past the windows toward the back of the house. As soon as she realized we could see her from the backyard, she came to a complete stop and looked our way. That's when it registered. It wasn't a teenage girl. It was Johnny's young wife, Shelia. And Shelia had a black eye."

7

"Three may keep a secret, if two of them are dead."
Benjamin Franklin

SHEILA SEEMED AFRAID AND RELUCTANT TO TALK TO US, BUT EVENTUALly, I convinced her to invite us in.

"How did you get that black eye?" Remy asked as soon as we had all introduced ourselves. "Do you need any medical attention?"

"No, I'm alright," Sheila replied. 'It's not the first time, but it will be the last. I won't let him do this to me again."

"Was it your husband? We might be able to help you."

Shelia looked at the floor. She couldn't have been more than twenty-five years old. Although she wasn't much younger than me, she was much younger than Johnny, who, according to Henrietta, was born in 1971. "We've been fighting lately about money," she said. "He keeps saying a big insurance payout is coming soon, that it will be a windfall, but there hasn't been any money yet. Only enough for temporary housing while everything is being investigated. He's starting to get nervous. He didn't realize that since his mother owns the house and the insurance policy, the insurance money will go to her. He thought we'd get it all." She shook her head in frustration. "At least Chet told him we'd get it all."

"Who's Chet?" Remy asked, the two of us exchanging a puzzled look.

"Chet Miller, Johnny's dumb high school buddy who finally managed to get out with his GED. He got lucky. His aunt got him an important gig with some place that works with insurance companies. He knew we would get paid if our house burned down. He made it sound like we'd get plenty for the house and all our stuff. They would put us up in a nice hotel while we decided whether or not to rebuild. Chet promised to help us navigate it all with the insurance company, but it's a big mess. Chet is in jail now, and we're hurting for money."

"Shelia, are you saying the three of you made plans to set the house on fire?" I asked.

"Oh God, no! I would never do that. Neither would Johnny."

"Really?" I said. "Let me ask you this: how long after this conversation took place did the house catch fire?"

"A few months, I think. Johnny and Chet talked a lot about it, but it had to be a coincidence. Johnny is a lot of things but he's no criminal."

"We're talking about the same Johnny who gave you that black eye right?" Remy asked. Shelia looked away and started to cry.

"Shelia," I said, my voice gentle, "let's sit down, and you can tell us everything you know, beginning with what happened the day of the fire. From all accounts, it started at around 3:30 a.m., but nobody was home. Where were you?"

As the three of us sat at the breakfast table. Shelia told her story. "The week before the fire, Johnny was talking about us getting away for a few days. He has kids with his two prior wives, but we were planning on having at least one of our own. He thought us being away for a few days without his kids would be fun. We checked into a hotel in Buckhead the evening of the fire and had a nice dinner, but Johnny was distracted."

"What do you mean?" Remy asked. "Distracted by what?"

"He was texting throughout dinner. He also left the table a few times to take some calls, which he never does. When I asked him what was going on, he said he had some business to take care of at his plumbing job, but it was no big deal.

"Before we left for the hotel, he started acting weird. I thought he was drunk. He asked the server to take pictures of us at the table. He never does that either.

"When we got back to the hotel, we went to the bar for a toast. He said something about 'to new beginnings.' It was strange, but I felt good about it, thinking he was excited about possibly expanding our family.

"We went to bed late that night, then were woken early by our neighbors and the fire department, calling to say our house was on fire."

She started crying again, but this time it was heavy and sorrowful. "He couldn't have been a part of this!" she said. "There's just no way," But after sharing her story out loud, her mind knew what was weighing on her heart. Her husband was a part of this in a big way. Just talking with Shelia, though, I knew she wasn't a part of the plan.

Once Sheila composed herself, I asked her why she was here at the Carnes house. "Johnny isn't himself. He's nervous and tense and taking it out on me. She pointed to her black eye. I'm not going to put up with that anymore! I get along well with the Carnes, so they gave me a spare key several months ago for emergencies. I knew they would be out of town for a while, so I spent last night here. I'll likely stay for another week while my eye heals, then head to my parents' house in Alabama. I could never let them see me like this. My father would come for Johnny."

I felt sorry for her, but there wasn't much more to say. We exchanged contact information, and I let her know the police would be in touch for an official statement, that she was a key witness to a potential crime. I also let her know there would be no big insurance payout for her and Johnny. This was no accidental fire.

"This is what we call insurance fraud and arson," Remy added, though she probably shouldn't have. "Somebody will do time for it."

We were careful not to say anything as we walked out the door. Henrietta was still out and about, and we didn't want her to overhear us. It wasn't until we got back in the van that we looked at each other in amazement. Remy kicked things off. "So, Johnny lets his high school friend, Cooter—"

"Chet," I interjected. She always called people she didn't know but knew she didn't like "Cooter." It was an inside joke.

"Chet, Cooter, same difference. Johnny was dumb enough to set his own mother's house on fire because his buddy had a spoonful of information about insurance claims. He put his entire life and family in jeopardy, and now he knows it. There's no doubt he'll face prison time. He must be desperate."

Remy was about to call Detective Jefferson to let him know what we discovered when I realized we had forgotten to ask Shelia what company Chet worked for, so I went back to ask while Remy made the call.

"Shelia, I'm sorry to intrude again," I said. "I appreciate all the help, but I have one more question. Where is Chet Miller employed?"

Shelia thought about it, then told me she didn't know.

"What kind of company is it?" I asked. "He told Johnny he works with insurance companies. Could it be an auto body shop?"

She shook her head.

"A law firm?"

Another no.

"What about a construction company?"

"I'm sorry," she said. "I wish I knew more, but Johnny never said the name."

"Don't worry about it. We'll find out. Have a good one." I didn't show it, but I was disappointed.

As I turned to leave, I thought of one more question, so I turned back before Sheila could close the door. "Excuse me, but you mentioned Chet's aunt got him the job. Do you know her name?"

She thought for a moment. "I think it's Maple or Marie or something. No, it's Marge. Johnny joked that when they were younger, some of the mean kids would call her names behind her back. I never saw her, but she must be heavyset."

"Why do you say that?"

"The mean kids called her 'Large Marge.'"

I almost fell off the porch, but somehow I managed to keep my balance. When I reached the van, Remy was still speaking with Detective Jefferson. I told them both what Shelia had just shared. Jefferson advised us not to say or do anything differently with Wilson or his girlfriend, Marge. They would investigate them right away and get back to us. Remy and I sat in stunned silence. It was too much of a coincidence. If what we had just heard was true, Wilson, our trusted employee, might be involved in an egregious crime against us. Surely, we didn't have a traitor in our midst. Especially not him.

8

"I was restless, but finally found my way."
Emma Bonino

ROD'S FLIGHT WAS ABOUT TO TAKE OFF. ALTHOUGH IT WAS ONLY AN hour-long trip from Atlanta to New Orleans, he enjoyed a glass of Woodford Reserve. He was traveling in first class but was tired and wanted to calm himself. He hadn't been home in several months, and he planned to avoid his parents' questions about Remy. In fact, he decided to avoid them completely. It was too difficult for him to explain what had happened. He shook his head. Ironically, his parents thought the idea of owning an insurance company was risky. They were right, but they shouldn't have been. It could have been risky in a financial sense but not in terms of personal safety.

As the plane taxied toward the runway, he gave his empty glass to the flight attendant, then immediately fell asleep, thinking about how much he missed his wife.

He dreamed of her. They were at the opening of their new restaurant, the Sophia. It was a sophisticated event with friends and family in attendance. Everyone was formally dressed. Rod and Remy were holding hands and greeting guests from table to table. They were all having a good time, laughing, eating, and enjoying Creole food and music. Then Rod smelled smoke. Nobody else seemed to notice, but when he looked around, he realized smoke was pouring in from the exterior doors and windows. The restaurant was on fire!

He glanced toward Remy, but she was no longer there holding his hand. She was across the room, laughing with her sister and mother. He yelled for her, but she couldn't hear him. He continued shouting, telling everyone to get out, but no one moved.

He went to his parents and shook them, then Luke. They all just smiled while black smoke continued to fill the room. Rod ran to pull the fire alarm, thinking that would get them moving, but he could hardly see through the smoke. Then he heard screams.

Remy's dress was on fire. He looked into her fearful green eyes as he ran toward her, but he knew it was already too late.

Rod jolted awake as the plane's wheels touched down hard. As he looked around, the nightmare started to fade. He shook it off, then took a drink from the bottle of water he had stowed in the seat pocket in front of him.

When he reached the baggage area, still slightly shaken, he stopped for a second to listen to the jazz band playing nearby. Only in NOLA would passengers be treated to live music in that way. He was from a unique city. He nodded to the man playing the trombone, then placed a tip in the band's not-so-subtle tip jar.

At the rental car center, he settled into his black-and-white

BMW i8. Instead of driving east toward the heart of New Orleans, he took I-10 west toward West Baton Rouge. He sent a quick text to Detective Jefferson letting him know he was on the road, then stepped on the gas. The BMW i8 was his favorite sports car.

As soon as Rod had told Detectives Jefferson and Kinser that he was headed back home, they insisted he stay in touch throughout the visit. They didn't like the idea of him traveling while the case was ongoing. Rod understood, but insisted he needed some time away. He had agreed to check in with them daily, but he thought it was overkill. He wouldn't have been surprised if they had local police on standby if he got a nail in his tire.

His drive was almost an hour and a half. It was 5:00 p.m., which meant he'd get to his destination at around 6:30. Surely London would be done with her deposition by then. Maybe she would learn more.

Although it was rush hour, traffic was reasonable. Rod was driving just over the speed limit while listening to music. Almost every song reminded him of his best times with Remy. One of his favorites was the 1978 classic "What You Won't Do For Love" by Bobby Caldwell.

He was pulled back to the present when his GPS alerted him that his exit was one mile away. As he made his way over to the right lane, so did a dark Toyota SUV a few cars back. A second SUV did as well, but Rod didn't notice either of them. His mind was still caught up in the music, and his eyes were focused on the road ahead.

Once he took the exit, he was still about thirty minutes from his destination. He was a bit anxious because it was only winding back roads from that point onward. However, there was at least another hour of daylight.

As he drove, he encountered fewer and fewer cars. Eventually, the only vehicles on the road were his and an SUV that had been behind him for longer than he was comfortable with. When his GPS told him to turn right, he was tempted to turn left, but he didn't want to add more time to his drive, especially when he was probably just being paranoid.

Because of that paranoia, he reached into the center console and pulled out his Glock 19. It was the only reason he had checked his luggage at the airport. He had a permit to carry the gun in Georgia and Louisiana. The magazine was loaded with ten bullets. He carried a second magazine in his luggage, not that he expected to use it.

After a few more turns, the dark SUV was still behind him. Rod didn't like it, but he could outrun his tail easily and would do so if needed.

He made an unexpected U-turn to see what the SUV would do. It slowed down. Rod looked at the driver and saw he was white with a red scar over his left eye, clearly unhappy and quite surprised. Rod noted the SUV's license plate was partially covered. He gunned it and left the SUV in the wind.

"Shit!" he said. Who was following him in Baton Rouge? Whoever it was, it wasn't going to end well for them if they persisted. As he continued driving in the opposite direction of his destination, which irritated him even more, he called Detective Jefferson.

"Jefferson!" Rod said, full of adrenaline. "You won't believe what just happened. Some idiot's been following me. I don't know what he wants, but I swear I'll blow his brains out if I have to!"

"I know, Rod. Calm down! I've had a tail on you since you left the airport. We spotted the guy in the SUV and have been following you both. You probably didn't see us because we stayed far enough behind him, but we've been with you this whole time. I suspect you have your gun out. For God's sake, put that thing away, and let us deal with it. Hold on . . . It sounds like they have him pulled over right now." Jefferson paused as he received a sitrep on his other phone. "He doesn't have any ID on him. We don't know who he is yet or his purpose, but we'll find out. He's not going anywhere. You're good to turn around and head back as planned. You'll see the flashing lights. Keep going, and we'll have an escort behind you. That's the least we can do."

Damn right, Rod thought, though he knew how hard the detectives were working to solve the case. "Alright. I'm turning around now, but tell your people I'm late. I'm gunning it from here on out." He disconnected the call and made up for lost time.

When Rod reached the flashing lights, he slowed and saw the SUV driver in handcuffs on the side of the road as the police searched his vehicle. Rod had no idea what they would find—probably plenty linking him to no good—but he was just glad to be free of it. He didn't care if he had a police escort. He hit the gas with only one thing on his mind.

9

"If you live to be a 100, I want to live to be a 100 minus one day so I never have to live without you."
Winne The Pooh

AN HOUR LATER AS ROD PULLED UP TO A SMALL BUT CHARMING HOUSE, the sun was beginning to set, and the porch light was on. Although he couldn't see through the closed plantation shutters on the two front windows, he could tell the lights were on inside too. It was an architectural-style shotgun house, common in many parts of Louisiana. The home was narrow with rooms connected one behind the other with one exterior door at each end of the house. It got its name with the idea that if a bullet was shot from the front or back door, it could travel straight through the house without hitting anything else.

Rod got out of the car and walked up the porch steps carrying his overnight bag. He looked around and didn't see any signs of the police car he had outrun. His heart was racing. It had been a long time.

He was about to knock on the front door when it opened. Within the warm glow of the lights behind her, he finally saw his wife, Remy, for the first time in weeks. Her maroon-highlighted hair hung straight to her shoulders, and she was wearing a simple sleeveless blue dress with sandals. She was perfect.

"Well, it's about time, handsome. I wondered if you'd ever get here!" Remy said as she jumped off the porch and into her husband's arms. They held each other for a long time, Remy's head fitting perfectly into the crook of Rod's neck. Then they released each other and walked inside, holding hands just as the police cruiser pulled up. Rod gave him a wave of acknowledgment and then closed the front door.

The house smelled like his favorite candle scent, Suede and Smoke, and something else he couldn't put his finger on. Remy knew him well.

"I missed you," he said as he held her again.

"I missed you more. Thank God you're here."

They shared a passionate kiss, something they hadn't been able to do in a while but needed desperately. Finally, they pulled apart.

"I bet you're hungry," Remy said.

"I am but not for food."

"Hmm . . . I like that, Rod. But I have something special for you. Lots of special things."

Remy smiled and then led him down the singular hallway toward the back of the shotgun house toward the kitchen. That's when the other scents hit him. He smelled some of his favorite foods, which only Remy knew how to cook just right. The crab cakes were baking in the oven while the shrimp were sautéing in a succulent tomato-based sauce. The pasta looked like it was almost ready. His mouth watered, and his stomach growled, reminding him he hadn't eaten anything since he left Atlanta earlier that afternoon. The love they shared had seemed to grow over the past few weeks since Remy "died."

"You can't imagine how heartbreaking it is to have so many people think you're dead. I can't go anywhere without someone expressing their sympathy. With so many thinking you're dead, it's hard to leave the house, not to mention go to work."

"I know. It's terrible. But we just have to wait a bit longer until these criminals make another mistake."

Thinking Remy was right, Rod held her tighter. After a month, the detectives were still trying to put the pieces together. Someone had run Remy off the road and flipped her car. The only thing they knew for certain was that she was followed from the second fire scene when she went back without London. They thought the events were connected, but they didn't know that for sure.

Right after the crash, Remy remembered hearing two men approach her vehicle, fearing she was dead. It was clear they intended to kidnap her and knew this would not go over well with the "boss." They had no choice but to leave, thinking she was dead.

The police suggested Remy stay away under the pretense that she died in the car accident. Their hope was the perpetrators would attempt another kidnapping within the family since the first one failed. The detectives talked London into accepting a protective detail, but Luke had refused.

The only people they knew who were directly connected were the arsonist, Chet Miller, who was already in jail, and his low-ranking partner, Johnny Lott. Chet still wasn't talking. Johnny had talked, but he was only connected to Chet. He didn't know anything other than what Chet told him.

After four weeks, it seemed less likely the police would connect the dots anytime soon. As they ate, Rod and Remy agreed they could not keep up this pretense. Rod was bringing his wife home where she belonged. This situation wasn't good for anyone, especially them.

They decided to call the detectives in the morning. They were thrilled to be together and didn't want to spend their time talking about the case. Rod didn't mention his tail from earlier. He would ask more about it when he spoke with Jefferson in the morning. But he knew his wife and was curious about something.

"Remy, does your mother know you're alive?"

She smiled slyly. "What makes you ask that?"

"Well, she didn't seem nearly as upset as I would expect if her firstborn daughter died in a car accident in the prime of her life."

"London told her everything from the beginning. We agreed that if we were going to do this, there was no way we would put our mother through it. She knows I'm okay. She just doesn't know where I am. That's why Luke urged us all to get Mom out of town all this time. She's spending time with our cousins in California."

When they finished dinner, it was still early, but time was meaningless to them. While Remy went to the bedroom, Rod checked the locks on the front and back doors. He peeked through the shutters and saw the police cruiser was there in front of the house too. On his way back through the house, Rod took in the home. It was beautiful with thick old-world baseboards and molding throughout.

As Remy changed, she reflected on how the solitude had allowed her guilt-free time to focus on herself and to think. Rod was her soulmate. She believed everyone had a soulmate but only a few were fortunate enough to find them. Tonight, she would show him how she felt in ways she had not done before.

When Rod entered the bedroom, he couldn't believe his eyes. He had thought Remy was stunning before, but now she was wearing lingerie that left nothing to the imagination. She was standing in front of a large mirror on the wall with a thick, ornate frame that highlighted her in every way. He knew he was blessed beyond measure. She was alive, unharmed, and she was his.

They locked eyes, not needing to say another word. For the first time, he realized music was playing. It was one of his favorite Regina Belle songs from 1989, "Baby Come to Me." He closed the door and then did exactly what he longed to do for the past four weeks.

While Remy and Rod enjoyed their reunion, in the shadows across the street someone was lurking. He was masked and had waited for over an hour for darkness to fall and the police officer to get out of the vehicle. When the officer got out to stretch his legs, turning to face the house, the stranger rushed up behind him.

Sensing his presence, the officer turned around, but it was too late. The masked man pounced and shot him in the chest, a silencer muffling the blast. There was no fight. The officer tried to yell a warning, but it came out as a whisper. Collapsing into the gunman's arms, his body went limp as he was dragged around to the driver's side of the cruiser.

After pausing to make sure no one was around, the masked man opened the rear door and shoved the officer's body inside. If someone passed by, they wouldn't see anyone in the car. The man took the officer's gun, radio, and Taser. Now he was ready to go after his real target. He just had to wait for the right moment.

10

"What's normal anyways?"
Forrest Gump

I WAS BECOMING EDGY. MY DEPOSITION HAD BEGUN JUST AFTER 2:00 p.m., and we were resuming after another break as the clock struck 7:00 p.m. I told Robert I was mentally exhausted. I knew the Taylor brothers had many more questions, but I was done for the day. They had interviewed Detective Jefferson and had what they needed to defend their client. I wondered who was defending Johnny Lott. I also wondered what they were hoping to get from me.

Robert seemed relieved to approach the Taylor brothers, letting them know five hours was long enough for us both. I looked at my watch, realizing that Rod was already with

Remy. I hoped they were able to block out the whole world and focus only on each other. It warmed my heart to think of those two reuniting. I couldn't wait to see my sister again. It was difficult living under the pretense of Remy being dead, but the detectives thought it would draw out whoever had tried to kidnap her. They also believed they could protect us better this way. Luke and Rod had their doubts about that, but what did any of us know about police protection?

"Gentlemen, this deposition is over," Robert said. "We believe five hours of testimony is sufficient to comply with the subpoena. If you have any additional questions, I suggest you put them in writing and send them to my office for review."

Alexander and Joey weren't happy, but their hands were tied. I had been subpoenaed, and I had complied. If they wanted more, it wouldn't be in that ultra-plush, intimidating downtown office. And goodness knows I didn't need more hours of sitting across from Alexander and his brother.

"You know we didn't have a chance to talk about Remy," Joey said as we gathered our things, "although I understand it's a very difficult subject. London, again, I'm sorry for your loss, but we need to learn more about what happened."

I had no intention of responding, but even if I had, Robert would have cut me off. "As I just stated," he said, "you can forward any additional questions to my office. We're done here."

We headed for the door, but it was a little too abrupt for me. None of this seemed normal. I stopped and turned around. "Thank you, everyone. Have a good evening."

Once we were out in the hallway, I was hoping to make a clean getaway, but Alexander's long legs soon caught up to us. "London! Wait."

Robert and I stopped and turned around to face him.

"I can't believe you walked out like that. It's been a year since we last saw each other. Don't you think we should talk?"

"We did talk."

"Oh, come on. You know what I mean."

I knew what he meant, but it had been a long day, and I

wasn't in the mood. Plus, Robert was there and was way too curious to hear what we had to say. "Let's talk tomorrow or next week. I'll call you."

The look on his face said he wasn't convinced I would.

"Tell you what," I continued. "I'll call your assistant and put something on the calendar for us. That will be the easiest way."

We both knew that wasn't going to happen either, but instead of him objecting like I thought he would, he just nodded. "Thanks, London. It was good seeing you." He turned and walked back toward the conference room. Why did I feel so badly about that?

Robert gave me a bewildered look.

"We should go," I said before he could ask whatever he was going to ask.

We walked the short distance to the elevator and then waited in silence. We made it past the lobby, where my detail was waiting and into the parking lot before Robert spoke his peace. "By the way, I think it's love."

I gave him a puzzled look. "What are you talking about?"

"When Alexander first saw you, he was completely enthralled. It was obvious he was feeling something, but now after spending five hours with him and seeing how he interacted with you, I have no doubt the man is still in love with you."

"Trust me, he may feel some kind of way about me, but it isn't love. This I know for sure."

Robert wasn't convinced, but we said our goodbyes as I got in my car. We agreed to talk the following day. I looked into the rearview mirror and, true to form, my escort was behind me.

Thankfully, traffic died down. It was an easy drive home. I thought about what Robert said, but when Xander and I ended things, he didn't want to see me again. I called him several times, but he wouldn't return my calls or texts. I hadn't wanted things to end the way they did, but he didn't give me a choice. We both had tried to move on, dating other people. I wasn't dating anyone now, and I had no idea if he was or not. I convinced myself it didn't matter anymore.

I was lost in thought when Luke's name appeared on my dashboard. He had texted me earlier, but I didn't have a chance to text him back. I accepted the call, and his animated voice filled the car. "Hola, sis. How did it go? It's been over five hours."

"I know. I was there! I'm completely drained, but aside from that, it wasn't too crazy. Alexander wasn't nearly the 'Pitbull' he could have been. We ended it before they started asking about Remy, and I didn't have to perjure myself. Thank goodness that's over. I'm sure they'll send written questions. But who cares? By then it may be a moot point."

"I think you're right. The case against their client is open and shut. Surely, you know they didn't need to depose you. I think today was just a fishing expedition. I suspect a part of it was your ex-fiancé flexing his muscles and his brother agreeing to it. It was an easy way for Alexander to see you after all this time."

"Why would you think that?"

Luke hesitated. "Well, I ran into him a few months ago before all this went down. He asked about you."

"What did he want to know?"

"The usual. How you were doing, were you happy, were you seeing anyone."

"Luke, I can't believe you didn't tell me! What did you say?"

"Not a whole lot. Just that you were good, you were doing great personally and professionally."

"Why didn't you tell me?"

"Would it have made a difference?"

"Nope. Not at all."

"That's why."

"Fair enough," I said, though I thought most men, including my brother, had half a brain. If my besties or Remy ran into Alexander, they would have called me immediately and told me everything word for word. "I get it. I'll text you when I get home. Love you."

Alexander and Joey sat alone in the conference room. They were both deep in thought but for different reasons.

"I wanted to get more from London," Joey said. "But at least she clarified why the police started looking into our client. It began unraveling for Chet when she and Remy went to that fire scene and found his buddy's wife. If that loser Johnny hadn't hit her, she would have never been at the neighbor's house that day. Man, I hope she presses charges against him. He was arrested for arson but was lucky to get bail with help from his mother."

Alexander didn't respond, too caught up in the aftermath of the deposition. He couldn't believe London had just brushed him off. She'd get on his calendar. What kind of bull was that? They had been engaged and almost married. They should be married right now, celebrating their first anniversary. He had tried to get over her, even dated a little. They were good women, but when they wanted to take things to the next level, he wasn't interested and ended it. He knew why, but he never wanted to admit it, not even to himself. The truth was, he was still in love with London. He thought it would lessen over time if he refused to talk to her, but social media was a beast. He visited her profiles and saw she had deleted most of the pictures with him but not all. The ones with their families and special occasions stayed on but nothing else with just the two of them.

What did he expect? She had left him the night before their wedding. Seeing her had brought it all back, like being hit with a slow bullet. She was beautiful, smart, and funny. He wanted to pull her out of that conference room and take her back to his office to remind her of what she'd been missing. He was glad Joey brought him back to reality when he first saw her. When she left, everything fell apart for him. If not for

Joey, he would probably still be struggling.

Despite everything, she had called him "Xander" before the deposition. London was the only person who did. He remembered a night they had a fight about something insignificant. She was upset with him and said, "What. Ever. Alex. An. Der." For some reason, her pronunciation of his name was funny to him. He started laughing and couldn't stop. London didn't want to laugh, but laughter is contagious and before they knew it, they were both cracking up. They made up in every way possible and ever since then, she had called him Xander. He couldn't help but smile at the memory that only the two of them shared.

"Bro, did you hear me?"

"What's that? Right. She should press charges."

"Oh, crap," Joey said.

"I knew we were taking a chance bringing her up here. She had you as soon as she walked into the room. I could see it in your eyes. You still have it bad for her."

"No, JT, I'm good," Alexander said. "I was just thinking about everything she laid out. Nothing more. With everything she shared, one thing stumped me."

"What's that?"

"I know it's been over a year, but I think I'm pretty good at reading London. I didn't see the reaction I thought I would when we brought up her sister. Remy was killed just over a month ago, but London barely flinched when we offered our condolences. They were close. That's not normal for her."

Joey thought about it and then shrugged. "It's been a while. Maybe you don't know her as well as you think you do anymore."

"I guess you're right." But Alexander didn't agree. His gut told him something was off.

Before the brothers left the office, one of their new junior attorneys, Haley Steel, knocked on the door. She hadn't witnessed any of the depositions that day, but she wanted to disclose something.

"Come on in," Joey said. "I'm surprised you're still here."

Haley walked in but wasn't her cheerful, confident self. They both sensed something was off. Haley was a smart, attractive woman with short, fiery-red hair, and she showed lots of potential at the firm.

"I'm sorry to bother you after you've been in depositions all day. But when I saw the attorney representing London Devereaux, I knew I had to say something."

That got Alexander's attention. "Say something about what?" he asked.

"I'm a little embarrassed to share this, but, well, Robert Young and I dated for two years. It was getting serious until I found out he was married. The signs were there all along, but I ignored them. When I confronted him, he reluctantly admitted it. I was heartbroken. Our relationship was no more than a long affair to him. He kept calling me after the breakup, trying to explain. Finally, I told him that if he didn't stop, I was going to tell his wife."

"What happened then?" Joey asked.

Haley looked up, holding back tears. "He stopped calling. I don't think he saw me today."

Neither Alexander nor Joey wanted to be the first to respond. They looked at each other, silently willing the other to speak. Since Haley wasn't involved in the case, there weren't any conflicts to address. She had shared her personal information. They appreciated that but didn't need to know anything more unless she made a harassment claim.

"Haley, I'm sorry you had to go through that," Alexander said. "I imagine it was hard to see him today. Thank you for bringing this to our attention. Is there anything you'd like us to do?"

"No. I just wanted you to know in case he *did* see me or said something," she said.

Alexander advised her to let them know if anything came of it and agreed she would work on other cases that didn't involve Robert or DSIG.

She thanked them and walked then out of the office.

Joey got up to close the door. "The squeaky-clean Robert Young, Esquire, was cheating on his wife for two years and thought he could get away with it. How ironic that she works for us. I wonder how he would have handled seeing her today. Unbelievable!"

"I don't like that guy, and now I know why," Alexander said.

Joey nodded. "Something tells me we might be able to take advantage of this."

11

"If you go for the knockout punch, you better know how to land it."
Author Unknown

WILSON SAID GOODNIGHT TO SERENA, ALL THE OTHER EMPLOYEES HAVing left for the day. Serena was in charge of doing the security sweep before locking up and setting the alarm at night. Her law enforcement background made her the perfect closer. She was the type of person to assume there would be trouble even where there wasn't any. Once they exited the building, they went their separate ways.

Although he wasn't thrilled about going home, Wilson had to talk to Marge about her disdain for London and her family. She knew how much he enjoyed his job and the close relationship he shared with the Devereauxs, and she hated it.

He had ridden his bike to work, but instead of riding it home, he walked alongside it, thinking of what he would say to her. As he made his way to his tree-lined street, a police car rolled up on him—no flashing lights, just the cop car. Before the door opened, he recalled a few weeks earlier when Detectives Jefferson and Kinser had pulled up alongside him on his walk home from work.

They took him to a park to "chat," as they called it. He had no idea Marge's nephew Chet worked at her construction company, much less that he was one of the arson suspects. He was shocked when they told him. It was unthinkable. After a lengthy conversation, Wilson had convinced the detectives that he didn't know anything, and he agreed to cooperate with their investigation. If something unusual happened, he would alert them. He left that conversation shaken and knew he had to leave Marge soon.

"Wilson," one of the officers said as he got out of the car. He was a young, stocky Hispanic man with a buzz cut. Wilson didn't recognize him, but he knew they were there about Marge.

"Hello, officer. What can I do for you?"

"I'm Officer Lorenz. I'm helping the detectives working the DSIG arson fires." He put his hands on his hips—no handshake offered. "We haven't heard from you in a while. Are you holding out on us?"

"No, of course not."

"Then tell me what's going on with your girlfriend. What has she been saying about DSIG and her nephew now that he's been arrested?"

Wilson doubted the police were on the right track with their investigation. Marge had her issues, but she couldn't have known about or supported any of this. She had told him and the police she had no idea Chet was dumb enough to commit felonies for profit, although he had always gotten into trouble as a teenager. She was trying to do right by her family and gave him a job. No more, no less. That conversation between him and Marge had occurred weeks ago and ended with her being hurt and angry. She couldn't believe he dared to suspect her.

Wilson told Lorenz about his conversation with Marge earlier that day. She was still upset that DSIG wasn't referring her construction company to its customers. But she seemed more offended than usual. She indicated London should have learned her lesson from the fires and Remy's passing, but she never discussed it at home. In fact, since that first conversation, Marge was a little quieter about the Devereaux business than usual.

Officer Lorenz nodded. "Alright, Wilson. Stay connected with us. Don't let another week go by without talking to one of the detectives. If you get a bad feeling about anything else, give us a call. You understand me?"

"Yes of course, officer. I'll absolutely call. You have my word."

"Here's my card." The officer handed it to him. "If you can't reach Detectives Jefferson or Kinser, call me."

Wilson took the card and put it in the kangaroo pocket of his hoodie.

Once the cruiser pulled away, Wilson started walking his bike again. He saw his townhouse across the street, just two houses down. Wilson looked around to see if anyone was watching. Although there were plenty of streetlights, it wasn't exactly daylight. Someone could be watching in the shadows.

As he continued his short walk, he didn't realize he was the center of attention by more than the police. Serena had seen it all. They had left in opposite directions when they departed DSIG, but she was curious about the eccentric manager, so she followed him. She was close enough to hear some of the conversation with Lorenz and wasn't surprised to hear he was sharing what he knew about Marge. She decided to continue following until he got home.

While Serena was tailing Wilson, Marge was watching from a second-floor window in their home. The townhouse was close enough for her to see his encounter with Lorenz, but she couldn't hear what was said. Marge didn't know what was going on, but she didn't like it. She planned to have a conversation with Wilson that night.

Wilson was about to put his key in the front door when Serena appeared beside him.

"Holy cow!" he exclaimed, nearly dropping his key. "What the hell are you doing here? Did you follow me home?"

"Shh! Keep it down! No, of course not. Well, yes, but that wasn't my intent. I just wanted to see what you were up to."

"What I was up to? Are you kidding me? I'm going home after a long day at work. That's what I'm up to."

She motioned him away from the door. "I saw you talking to the police," Serena whispered. "And so did Marge."

That stopped him cold. "What do you mean?"

"I was watching when the police rolled up on you. Then I saw Marge looking out of an upstairs window. The lights were on at first, but she turned them off so she could watch without being seen."

Wilson hung his head. "No, no, no. This can't be happening! She's not supposed to know I'm talking to the police."

"Well, she knows now. Just tell her something close to the truth. She can't be surprised that the police would want to talk to you."

Wilson raised his head, looking Serena in the eye. "You're right. Marge shouldn't be surprised, and I didn't do anything wrong. If my cooperation with the police bothers her, she needs to look within herself to figure out why. Her nephew committed a crime against the company I work for. I'm done tiptoeing around her. She can get out of my house for all I care. I don't need this anymore."

His voice was rising, so Serena tried to reel him back so Marge wouldn't hear him. "Okay. I know what you mean. You're ready to face her and give her the knockout punch. Do you want me to stick around just in case?"

"Thanks, Serena, but no. I'm fine. I've never felt better." He lowered his voice again as he looked around. "I'm ready to end things. I've never been more certain of anything in my life."

Serena nodded. "I can tell you mean it. I'll get out of your hair. Good luck! I'll see you tomorrow."

Wilson watched her jog away. Then he took a deep breath and unlocked the door. He was determined things with Marge would end that night.

As soon as he entered the foyer, he called out for Marge, but there was no response. He found her sitting with a glass of red wine at the round kitchen table.

"I saw you, Wilson," she said, her words slightly slurred. "First with the police and then with a woman. Was that your girlfriend out there? Are you so disrespectful that you'd bring another woman here to our home?"

He took a closer look at her. He saw something different in her eyes. Was it regret, hurt, honesty?

"No. I would never bring another woman here. The distance between us has nothing to do with another woman. I have never cheated on you. Ever."

She nodded in acknowledgment. "Then who is she?"

He paused, wanting to keep his answer as concise as possible. "Oddly enough, it was our receptionist, Serena. She was nosy and wanted to know where we lived. Now I need to know something from you. Did you have anything to do with those fires that Chet set?"

Still feeling high from his conversation with Serena, when Marge didn't answer, he pushed. "Don't think of feigning outrage with me. Just tell me the truth."

She poured herself another glass of wine before replying. "You need to know? I'll tell you what you need to know. Everybody isn't in love with the perfect Devereaux family! It could have been anybody—the clients whose claims they deny, the employees who don't agree with their business model, and people who don't like you. That's right you, their loyal manager might have enemies too. Oh, and let's not forget that London dumped that good-looking lawyer of hers. Maybe he's behind it. It wouldn't surprise me at all!"

"I'm going to ask you one more time," Wilson said, refusing to take the bait. "Are you involved?"

"No, Wilson, I'm not. But I wish I had been!"

That set him off. Wilson knew he was losing control, so he took a step back, though he was still close enough to point his finger in her face. "Get out! You have ten minutes to pack up whatever you can and leave. Don't come back. We'll make arrangements for you to get whatever is yours another time. I don't want anything to do with you ever again." He clenched his teeth. "Do you understand?"

"What? Are you serious? You need me. You think that family cares about you, but they don't. I'm all you have. We can work things out."

Wilson shook his head, holding fast. "No, Marge. Go upstairs and pack. You need to leave."

Suddenly, her demeanor changed. "Oh, so you finally grew a pair. I'll leave alright. But on my terms."

Marge leapt toward him, wine bottle in hand, and smacked it into Wilson's temple. He stumbled back, almost falling to the floor. Marge hit him again, this time breaking the bottle. This time he went down.

Marge jumped on top of him. With the weight of her on his back, Wilson didn't have a chance. She started choking him. He heard her shouting but was losing consciousness, unable to make out what she said. As much as he tried to fight back, he couldn't. He was getting weak. He managed to touch the left side of his head and felt something sticky. Then his world faded away.

12

"The only thing worse than a liar is a liar that's also a hypocrite."
Tennessee Williams

ONLY WHEN MARGE GOT OFF HIS BACK DID SHE REALIZE WHAT SHE HAD done. "Oh my God! Wilson! Wake up. I'm so sorry!" She tried to wake him up, but he wasn't moving. "Wilson, please wake up. I love you, sweetie!"

She turned him over and was taken aback when she saw the big gash she had created on the side of his head. There was a huge red mess on the floor. Marge was at a loss. She knew their relationship was strained, but she didn't realize he had been ready to end it. To kick her out.

When she saw Lorenz's card, which had fallen out of his hoodie pocket, her emotions flashed from grief to anger. "You bastard!" She kicked him on the side. "I hate you, Wilson! You made me do this. This is all your fault! I hate you!" She kept kicking and cursing until there were no more words, just screams.

Exhausted, she paced back and forth in their galley kitchen for thirty minutes, trying to calm down and figure a way out of the situation. In between fits of grief, it finally hit her. She grabbed her cell phone from the table and found the number listed under "Marty." She didn't know his real name, but she called him that because he reminded her of the main character from her favorite Netflix series, *Ozark*. The beloved character, Marty Byrde, was part father figure, part criminal, and part genius.

They had only spoken a few times. He was always so relaxed, even though his voice was distorted by software. The first time he had called her with a proposition, he seemed to know all about her—the failing construction company, tax problems, her relationship with Wilson, and how cruel others were for making fun of her weight for so many years. He also knew of her strong dislike for the Devereauxs. And he had taken advantage of it all. She assumed he was a man, but she didn't know for sure. How could she have been so stupid?

According to "Marty," the plan was simple. He provided multiple addresses. She would choose which houses and arrange the arsons. He paid her for each one. He never said why and only set a few parameters. At first, it was just one fire. But that number increased when it didn't have the impact on DSIG that Marty had hoped. He knew the fires would eventually be exposed as arson. That was intentional. She was intrigued. When he called back two weeks later, she laid out her plan to use her delinquent nephew, Chet. True to Marty's word, once the arsons took place, the money came quickly.

Marge hadn't expected Chet to get arrested, but once it happened, Marty told her he had anticipated it and arranged for Taylor & Taylor to take the case pro bono. They took one pro bono case per quarter. He called in some favors through a friend of a friend who convinced the brothers that Chet was innocent. They agreed to take the case.

Marty's calls were untraceable, but he had given her a number to call under dire circumstances. Marge considered this a dire circumstance.

As the phone rang, she tried to calm down. When it went to voicemail, as expected, there was only a beep, no message. She gave the short version of what had happened, and by the time she hung up, she was on the verge of a panic attack. Marge realized she had made two big mistakes. The first was killing her dear, sweet Wilson, and the second was confessing it all on a generic voice mailbox.

Luke was jumping into the shower when he heard his phone ring, so he let it go to voicemail. With Rod going to visit Remy for the first time in weeks, Luke was feeling reflective. What was he doing with his life? In his late thirties, he was doing well financially, but what else did he have? Casual acquaintances were fine, but that wasn't what he was looking for anymore.

When he got out of the shower, he saw a familiar number on his phone and almost ignored it. If she was calling him, she must be in a bad way. He listened to the message. She was pretty rattled, so he wasn't sure exactly what had happened, but he got the point. She was in trouble. Hesitant to call her back, he decided to text that he was on his way instead.

He made a few calls to get things started. He wasn't going to do the dirty work himself. Plus, he needed someone to meet them out there for her sake.

Once he was in the car, he realized London hadn't called him yet, so he gave her a ring.

"Luke, I'm sorry. I should have called you as soon as I walked in the door. I'm home, and all is well. The police are outside."

"Alright. I'm headed out. I'll talk to you soon."

"Everything okay? You don't sound like yourself."

"I'm good. I just have to make a quick run and take care of a few things."

"Okay. I'll let you go. Wait, have you heard from Rod?"

"No, and I don't expect to hear from him until tomorrow. Let them do their thing. We should be the last people on their minds right now."

"True. Maybe I'll call Remy tomorrow night if we don't hear anything by then."

After they hung up, Luke thought about all the madness that was swirling around them. He was the reluctant partner. His sisters were the ones who had wanted the insurance gig. His personal training business was extremely successful. He didn't need this additional distraction, but he had gone along with them mostly as a silent partner. They were starting to see a profit, but it was a roller coaster ride. It had likely contributed to the struggles he and his estranged wife Kelly had experienced. She thought it took too much time away from their time together. There were a lot of pressures, which wasn't a surprise. But they had no idea things would go so badly. Remy wasn't supposed to be run off the road and left for dead. That wasn't part of the plan. He loved his sister dearly. If he ever figured out who did it, they would be dead.

As Luke approached his destination, he saw a flurry of activity—flashing lights and cones on the road to divert traffic in both directions. He pulled over a few blocks away in his black Benz and watched. She was talking to the police. He hadn't seen her in person for a long time. She looked different, as if she were ready to handle her own affairs with or without his help. There wasn't much he could do at that point anyway. He decided to stay in his car to see how things played out.

Although she had looked strong at first glance, he realized she was shaking. It was still warm from the early summer heat, but the officer gave her a thin blanket. That's when Luke finally got out of his car to find out what had happened. He couldn't stay incognito.

Luke walked up to her and the officer. As soon as she saw him, she grabbed him and hugged him. "Luke, thank God you're here!"

Damn, he thought. *This is not what I intended.*

13

"When you are in love, and you get hurt, it's like a cut—it will heal, but there will always be a scar."

Soo Jie

I SETTLED IN FOR THE NIGHT AND WORE MY JAMMIES, WHICH MEANT A T-shirt and shorts. I forced myself not to think much about it, but as I looked around my home, it was an eclectic blend of my and Alexander's tastes. Although we had broken up a year ago, he had never picked up the few odds and ends that were his. I thought about packing them up and having them delivered to him, but what was the point? He probably wouldn't accept them anyway, just like he hadn't accepted my calls.

My first-floor guest bedroom was filled with his dark,

masculine furniture. The kitchen island was paired with his barstools, and the worst part was his desk in my home office. I use it every day! I needed to get rid of that thing.

We had never officially lived together. After we got engaged, he spent most of his time at my place, a large five-bedroom house, and we started moving some of his things in. He was going to keep his three-bedroom home and rent it out. At least that was the plan—until it wasn't.

I relaxed on the sofa with a glass of cool chardonnay and reflected on the day. The quick prep with Robert, followed by the deposition and seeing Alexander, was almost too much. I had tried to prepare myself, but it was still a shock to see him. It was especially shocking to have him in my arms again. I hadn't expected that.

My life changed completely in a short period of time. Alexander and I dated for over a year before he proposed in a very dramatic way. We went out to dinner at an exclusive restaurant where it was almost impossible to get reservations. It was odd that the entire restaurant was empty. It was just us with the beautiful interior decorated as an indoor garden.

Shortly after we were seated, the server brought out champagne—my favorite. That was my second clue, considering we hadn't ordered any. Once it was poured, we toasted to our future. He took my hands in his and proclaimed his deep, overwhelming love. Before I knew it, Xander was on his knee with a princess-cut diamond ring larger than I could have ever imagined. When I said yes, the staff came out with more champagne, and our families and closest friends suddenly appeared from wherever they had been waiting. Between our mothers, his father, Remy, Luke, Joey, and many others there were lots of toasts, tears, and laughter. When I asked Xander what he would have done if I had said no, he said it never crossed his mind.

As we made wedding plans over the next twelve months, things were going well. We were madly in love and couldn't wait to spend the rest of our lives together. As for having a family, Alexander was up front and said he didn't see himself as a father. I knew he meant it, but I was naïve enough to think it was just a phase and at some point, he would want children. I always saw myself as a mother and couldn't imagine marrying someone who didn't want kids. But I was crazy about him and didn't want to face the possibility of what that meant.

As the wedding drew nearer, the conversation kept coming up, but his position never wavered. We were at an impasse. It wasn't something either of us was willing to compromise on.

"What are you going to do?" Remy asked before the rehearsal. "Imagine how awful it will be if you get pregnant. You'll be thrilled but only for a while. Knowing Alexander, he'll try to be happy, but you would bring a child into your marriage knowing it isn't what he wants. Or you'll never have a child, and at some point, you'll resent him because you will never get to be a mother because of him. I know it hurts, but either way, the love you share will have no way to grow because you want two different lives, even though you both want each other in them."

I had been struggling with the same issue for months. Here I was, an intelligent woman who didn't want to accept what I knew to be true.

Despite this inner conflict, the wedding rehearsal took place, as planned, the Friday before the big day. Before we headed to the rehearsal dinner, I told him we needed to talk.

"Baby, you seem so serious," he said as he pulled me onto his lap. "Why the sad face the day before our wedding?"

"Xander, this is so hard for me to say. I don't even want to say it out loud. But I think we both know we don't want the same things out of life. How can we possibly think our marriage will work when the vision of our future family is so different? We've been avoiding this topic lately because we know what it means, but we can't ignore it any longer."

"What do you mean?" Xander asked, urgency in his voice.

"You know what I mean. I want children, and you don't. I understand and respect how you feel, but it's not something we can compromise on."

"And you're bringing this up now? The day before our wedding?"

"We've been talking around it for a long time. It's been weighing on me for months."

"So, what do you suggest we do?" he asked.

"I need to ask you one last time what kind of life you want."

"I'm not perfect, so I don't expect perfection. I just want a life filled with love, respect, and laughter. I want the love we share to grow because I've never experienced anything like this with anyone else. I crave a life where I know you'll always be there as my partner, friend, and lover. I want to share everything with you. And in return, I'll be all those things for you. London, I love you with all my heart and don't want to spend any day, hour, or minute without you in my life."

Before I realized it, tears were running down my face as I remembered Alexander's words. I took a sip of wine. I wanted all those things too. We were in lockstep in every way except one—the most important one. I ended things that night, and I don't think he ever forgave me. As best man and maid of honor, Joey and Remy made the announcement to the waiting guests and family at the rehearsal dinner. We would not be there, but we wanted our guests to enjoy themselves as much as they could considering the circumstances. Everything was paid for, so they encouraged everyone to eat, drink, and dance the night away.

I cried myself to sleep that night and many more.

Alexander refused to talk to me for weeks. I tried to talk to him, but he blocked me, finding it too painful for him to talk to me. Both of us were broken for a long time. Perhaps we still were.

Alexander had been so preoccupied after the deposition that he almost missed his exit off the interstate. Once he made it home, he thought about what Joey said. Maybe it had been a mistake to subpoena London for the deposition. They had spoken once but hadn't seen each other since she broke things off the day before the wedding. She was the only one he ever wanted to share his life with, and she had cut him off at the knees.

There was no doubt they had been in love, but they hadn't come to terms with starting a family, and that was reason enough for her to end it. When she made the break, he removed her from his life. He had no intention of being friends. He wasn't capable of it. There was no question he could have handled the situation better, but for the sake of his sanity, he had to focus on other things, anything besides her. London had hurt him and then he had hurt her. Neither of them meant to do it, but they were far from perfect.

Their mothers stayed in touch and didn't let the breakup ruin their friendship. He had run into Mrs. Devereaux a few times at his mom's house. Both women hoped he and London would get back together. As for Alexander, he wasn't so sure.

For a long time, he tried to convince himself he was happy living without her, but after spending several hours with her at the deposition, he realized how much he still missed her.

Her smell, her smile, her voice, and even the way she rolled her eyes were almost too much in such a short period. He noticed the other guys checking her out. He was sure word had gotten out about the two of them.

Alexander decided to call his older brother, Gio. He always gave him good advice. Gio and his wife, Calli, had been married for six years and been together for almost ten.

Gio answered on the second ring. "Yo, what's up Alex? How did it go?"

"I'm not so sure. We didn't get anything to help our client, and if it wasn't for Joey, I would have made a fool of myself a few times. When I saw London, I couldn't help but go to her." Alexander laid everything out for Gio, explaining how seeing her had refueled everything for him, even though he had no idea how she felt about him.

Gio put Alexander on speaker so Calli could hear the conversation. "What does your heart tell you?" she asked. When Alexander didn't answer immediately. She continued. "Whatever your heart says, maybe you should follow that."

14

"I didn't come this far to only come this far."
Jesse Itzler

Rod kissed Remy and then got out of bed to check the doors one more time. On his way down the hall into the front room, he looked out the window. The police cruiser was still there. Then he stopped. Something still didn't feel right. He scolded himself for being paranoid. He was there with his beautiful wife, a police officer was out front, and the guy who had been following him earlier was in custody. He relaxed. All was well in his world.

The under-counter lights in the kitchen were still on. Rod decided to leave them on, so he could keep his bearings in case he needed to get up in the middle of the night.

On his way through the kitchen to check the back door, he saw movement by the window. "What the hell?"

No sooner had he spoken than a man dressed in dark clothing and a police face shield made of dark cloth rushed toward him. Rod reached for his gun, but, of course, he wasn't armed. Remy was only a room away. He would fight to the death to protect her.

Before he could attack, though, he felt excruciating pain as he was hit in the stomach by a Taser. Rod went down hard on his knees, then flopped onto his side. He tried to call out, but it came out as a gasp. He grabbed a kitchen chair and slammed it onto the floor, praying Remy would hear it. Then his body went rigid as the man tased him again.

Little did Rod realize, the man wasn't there to kill him. His orders were to take Remy and bring her to a location in Baton Rouge, then get out of town.

The man hurried out of the kitchen. He was unfamiliar with shotgun houses, but he realized every room was off the main hallway. If he went into one room and Remy ran out another, he would hear her. The only sound he heard, though, was Rod writhing on the floor. He paused and listened but didn't hear anything else.

The man looked around. All the doors were closed except for the one closest to the kitchen. He started there. It was a bedroom with two doors, one with light spilling from beneath it. He assumed it was a bathroom. When his eyes adjusted to the darkness, he didn't see anyone, but he knew it was the primary bedroom. Remy had to be in there. He held the Taser in his left hand and felt for the light switch with his right.

The lights came on, but there was no sign of Remy. He swept the room again, keeping an eye on the closed bathroom door. The other door was likely the closet. If she was in the house at all, she was behind one of those two doors.

"This doesn't have to be difficult!" he said. "I'm not here to hurt you or your husband. Just come out, so we can talk."

Remy heard his hollow words. Who was he, and why was he there? She had heard Rod's warning when he sent the chair crashing to the floor a minute earlier. She knew her husband, and she wasted no time jumping out of bed and finding a secure hiding spot.

She heard a police radio crackle. "Ken, come in. You out there, brother? Come in." The man cursed, and she knew if he had the police radio, the officer out front wasn't coming to save them. She knew not to say anything, to control her breathing, not to move at all.

The man turned the radio off, not wanting it to reveal his position in the house. He decided to check the bathroom first. He placed his hand on the knob and yanked the dark, heavy wooden door open. The bathroom had recently been renovated with black and white tile throughout. It had a large walk-in shower and a vanity with a single sink. Remy wasn't there. He opened the linen closet inside it just in case. She wasn't there either. It was too small. He walked out and closed the door, then looked across the room at the closet door.

It was the most obvious hiding spot. He almost smiled as he walked across the creaky hardwood floor, feeling proud of himself. This would be an easy paycheck.

Although he couldn't see Remy, she could see him, and her breath caught when she saw him coming straight toward her. Although she was frightened out of her mind, she forced herself not to swallow, afraid he would hear it—and her racing heartbeat. *Please don't let him see me. Don't let this man find me,* she prayed.

"Remy Devereaux, I'm coming for you," he said. "You got away from me once but not this time. I thought you were dead, but I was wrong. I should have climbed down that embankment when we ran you off the road, but I didn't have enough time. Tonight I have all the time in the world. I'll find you and take you away, or I'll kill your husband. It's your decision. Don't fight me!"

You mother f%$er!* Remy screamed in her mind. *You're the one who tried to kidnap me and almost killed me! How dare you?* Self-preservation made her calm down and study everything about him. Even though the bottom half of his face was covered, she memorized his brown eyes and pale skin. He was tall and thin but in good shape.

He snatched open the closet door and shoved the clothes. Nothing else was there. "Where are you, Remy?" he asked, tearing the clothes off the hangers. "I'm not stupid. I know some of these old houses have closets with hidden compartments in them. I'll find you. You better believe that!"

Remy started sweating, feeling the anger pouring off him. He was coming unhinged and was close to finding her. There was no doubt he would tear the room apart. She was there right in front of him, if only he had taken the time to look carefully. She and London would play hide and seek with their friends when they were children, and they were masters at hiding in plain sight. If she could stay still, like she did when they were kids, she had a chance.

She had discovered the hiding spot one day while she was bored and alone in the house. The police owned the safe house, and checked on her daily, but she doubted even they knew about it—at least none of the detectives had mentioned it. Suspecting she might need it one day, she practiced getting in and out of it at lightning speed. And it was a good thing. Now she was hiding there while her husband was incapacitated on the kitchen floor and a madman was just a few feet away from her.

The closet wasn't very deep, and he had already emptied it. He felt along the side walls to see if there were any hidden panels. Nothing. Then he knocked on the back wall. Thinking he felt something hollow, he tapped it again. Could the wall open to a hidden compartment? He banged on the wall, certain he was right. Then he felt it give a little toward the top.

He reached up and pulled the panel down from the top. It slid to about half the height of the wall, connecting to the closet in the next bedroom. *Aha!* he thought.

Remy remained still while he walked through the closet into the next bedroom. She wondered if she had enough time to get out of the bedroom, go to Rod, and get out of the house. But she thought it was unlikely considering she could hear the man searching for her in the next room.

As she weighed her options, Rod appeared in the bedroom doorway. He was moving fast considering he had just been tased. He didn't say anything, just put his finger to his lips as he looked around the room.

She realized Rod was looking for his gun, which had been on the nightstand. Now she was holding it in her damp right hand, a remote clutched in her other hand, ready to use both as needed. The sound of the man's movements was getting farther away, which meant he was looking into other rooms, but before Rod could take another step, the masked man headed back toward them. Then they heard a police siren in the distance.

"I see you recovered pretty quickly from the Taser," the man said from the hall just beyond the bedroom doorway. "You never know how long these things will incapacitate someone. I wasn't sent here to kill you, only to take your wife. Unfortunately, I can't seem to find her. Do you know where she is?"

"She must have made it out of the house while you were tasing me," Rod said. "She likely made it out the front door and ran to the police."

The man considered that. He didn't have much time. Hearing the sirens coming closer, he knew he had made a costly mistake by turning the police radio off. When they didn't get a response from the officer outside, they had probably put two and two together. Now he may not be able to deliver Remy. He hadn't gotten paid for the job yet, and worse, Remy might have escaped from the house.

Realizing he was running out of time, he drew his gun and pointed it at Rod. "Remy!" the man shouted. I'll kill your husband unless you leave with me now! If you can hear me, show yourself."

He was getting desperate. If Remy wasn't there, Rod would be his hostage.

15

"Desperation is like stealing from the Mafia: you stand a good chance of attracting the wrong attention."

Thomas Newman

"Someone hit me from behind," she said, holding onto Luke. "They tried to run me off the road into the embankment. When it didn't work, they took off!"

He was stunned. "Are you sure that's what happened?"

"Yes! I'm absolutely sure. They sped up on me and rammed into my rear bumper twice. I stepped on the gas, but I knew I couldn't outrun them. They drove off when the car spun in the middle of the street instead of crashing. The entire experience was like something out of a nightmare!"

"Ma'am, I'm sorry, but I need to get your full name again,"

the officer said.

"Of course. Kelly. Kelly Devereaux. This is my husband, Luke."

Luke was furious. It was almost exactly how Remy had described being attacked, except she was hit from the rear several times while it was raining. She couldn't control the car and flipped down the embankment on the side of the road. While trapped in the car, she heard and saw two men talking, looking down at her, but they weren't there to help. It took hours for the police and the paramedics to reach her. Miraculously, she escaped with just a few bruises. That's when the police came up with the idea of letting the assailants think Remy was dead. The hope was that they would reveal themselves by attempting an attack on London.

In light of this attack, Luke was starting to think the police were right. The arsons couldn't have been just about the business anymore. The attack on Remy and now this was unfathomable. Luke knew these were personal attacks, but against whom? Kelly or the entire family? No one seemed to know.

The police took Kelly's statement and indicated they would follow up with her the following day. Once they made the connection to the Devereauxs, they mentioned updating Detectives Jefferson and Kinser. Everyone knew this was not a typical hit-and-run. The towing company took Kelly's black Porsche Cayenne to the shop. She and Luke were ready to go, but where? They were still married, but they were separated and lived apart. Surely, she couldn't stay by herself, though. Maybe London would be open to having her over for the night. They'd been friends for a long time. He was about to call London, but Kelly interrupted him.

"Luke, will you please take me home? I'll file a claim with my favorite insurance company in the morning." She smiled when she said it. He could tell she was trying to keep things light, but she was still upset.

In that instant, he knew what he had to do. "We just need to stop by my place first to pick up a few things."

She tilted her head in puzzlement. "For what?"

"For me to get everything I need to stay at your house tonight—well, technically, our house." She was about to object, but he jumped in before she could. "Someone tried to run you off the road. I'm either spending the night at your place, or you're spending the night at mine. Either way, staying by yourself tonight is not a good idea."

"Alright. Good point. You can stay with me. No need for me to spend the night at your condo when we have much more room at my house. Oops, I mean *our* house." She made air quotes to emphasize her point. It was awkward. She wasn't sure what point she was trying to make considering it was *their* house. They were still married, and out of all the people she could have called, it only made sense to call him. She decided not to argue because as much as she didn't want Luke to know it, she needed him at that moment.

They drove back to Luke's place in silence. It had been months since they had last spoken. There wasn't much to discuss other than the incident. Kelly was aware of the arsons and what she originally thought was Remy's death, and she and London stayed in touch. London had introduced her to Luke years ago and was the maid of honor at their wedding.

They pulled into the garage and went inside. "I won't be long," Luke said. "Feel free to get something to drink or use the bathroom or whatever."

Kelly had never been to his place and was curious about the state of his household. She looked around the open, modern floor plan. It was reasonably clean and minimally furnished. She recognized a few pieces that Luke took when they split. The office had new furniture, along with a laptop, printer, and two monitors. It was a functional office and not just for show.

She noticed a pair of earrings on the coffee table. She didn't touch them, but she could see they were ladies' YSL gold hoops. She didn't have time to process her feelings about seeing them except that they belonged to another woman, and they were pricey. Luke reappeared with an overnight bag in hand. Then he went into his office and grabbed his laptop. "Ready?"

She glanced at the earrings again and then nodded. "Yep. Let's get out of here."

Kelly forgot Luke still had a key to their house, which he used to open the side door. He gestured for her to enter first, then followed her inside.

Now it was Luke's turn to take in the house. It was a 4,000-square-foot two-story home made of brick with a two-car garage. Although it was just the two of them, it had four bedrooms and three and a half baths. They bought it together before they got married four years ago. It was in a sought-after part of town called Roswell. He knew they'd make a good profit when they were ready to sell. He noticed Kelly had made a few subtle changes after he left.

Luke's phone interrupted their awkward silence. It was Detective Kinser. "Luke, I heard about Kelly. Is she alright?"

Luke gave her a quick once over. "Yeah. She'll be fine. I'm with her, but I don't like what's happening. First the arsons, then Remy, and now Kelly. Do you and Jefferson have any new leads on who the hell is targeting my family?"

"We do have some leads," Kinser assured him. "And we're following up on every one of them. We're working over a guy who was following Rod in Baton Rouge a few hours ago. He's been tight lipped, but he hasn't asked for an attorney yet, so we're going at him pretty hard."

"Wait. Somebody was following Rod in Baton Rouge? How did they know he was there?"

"We think someone's been following him around Atlanta, and they must have been watching him when he checked in for the flight. We're close to getting something out of him."

"What about my sister? Who's checking in on Remy?"

Detective Kinser was hesitant to answer. They were headed toward the safe house now because the patrol officer assigned to guard it wasn't responding. That could have been for several reasons, but Kinser had been concerned enough to send out multiple patrol cars.

"We're on our way to check on Remy now. I'm sure she's fine." He figured he sounded convincing enough, but at this point, Kinser wasn't sure of anything at all.

16

"I'm not quiet because I'm shy. I'm quiet because I'm dangerous."
Author Unknown

THE SIRENS WERE GETTING CLOSER.

"Damn it! Remy Devereaux. Where are you?"

"I told you. I think she made it out of here," Rod replied.

"I don't need your commentary! Shut up if you want to make it out alive."

Rod wanted to hurt this man. He had broken into the house where his wife had been safe for thirty days. It wasn't until Rod arrived that everything went downhill.

"How did you find us?" Rod asked.

"Oh, it was you. We kept an eye on you. For four weeks you didn't do much of anything. After the funeral, you went to work, you saw your in-laws, ran errands, and sometimes you went to DSIG and then back home. I should know. I followed you about seventy percent of the time. Talk about boring.

"When you left Atlanta, we followed you just to make sure Remy didn't rise from the dead, but then, sure enough, she did! The people I work for thought of everything, including the possibility of her being alive. I didn't think it was possible, but turns out it's true. That's why I'm here. I messed up that night. I made some mistakes. But guess what? Your wife isn't a cat. She doesn't have nine lives."

Rod wanted to kick himself. He had been determined to see his wife, and now they were both in jeopardy because of his selfishness. If anything happened to Remy, he knew he would kill the gunman. He had already tried to kill his wife once.

The sirens were right outside the front door. Time was up. The gunman knew they would find the police officer in the back seat of his cruiser. Taking Rod might be his only chance for survival. "Come with me. If I can't get out of here, you can't get out of here. You feel me?"

Rod nodded, doing his best to remain calm.

"Let's go. We'll leave by the back door. You stay in front of me, and don't make any fast moves. Now start walking—slowly."

While they walked those few precarious feet, Rod took advantage of the brief opportunity to interrogate the man. "Who hired you? Who's so determined to hurt my family? We're just normal people like everyone else."

"I asked the same question," the gunman replied. "Not that it matters to me, but I think you're dealing with a sick person who hates you or somebody in your family."

Rod pondered his words. None of them were angels, but they were honest, caring, people. Was someone out to seek revenge? If so, why?

"Enough talking," the man said. He had some respect for Rod, but he wasn't going to let that stand in his way of getting out alive and hopefully collecting the money that was owed to him.

As they made their way to the back door, the gunman peeked out the window. There were no red and blue lights. He couldn't see any police officers either, but he knew they would circle the house in a matter of minutes if they hadn't already.

He shoved his gun into Rod's back. "Open the door, and keep your hands where I can see them. If you do anything crazy, I will shoot you." The truth was, he needed Rod walking, talking, and alive. If Rod went down, it was over for the gunman too.

Remy heard it all as the two of them walked out of the bedroom and into the hall. Once she was sure they were in the kitchen and out of earshot, she used the remote she was clutching in her hand to open the large built-in door. She had been hiding for what seemed like forever inside the huge mirror, which was six feet high and two feet deep and built into the wall. Whoever had built the hideaway was ingenious. She had been terrified she would be found but calmed a little when the man focused on the closet instead of the mirror, which seemed to be hanging on the wall. She was able to see everything through the one-way glass. Remy couldn't believe that just hours earlier, Rod had studied her in front of that same mirror, taking in her beauty.

Now that she was out of her hiding place, Remy had a decision to make. She could run out the front door away from the madman and into the safety of the police, or she could follow the gunman and her husband to the back door and try to save Rod. It was an easy choice.

She knew Rod was trying to be casual, but she could hear the strain in his voice as he and the gunman talked. She tiptoed into the kitchen behind them. Rod opened the door to an immediate police response. Seconds before it had been dark and quiet outside, now flashing lights were everywhere.

"Jasper Stone, come out and show your hands!" a voice

said over a loudspeaker.

The man, Jasper, cursed as he slammed the door. "I'm not going back to prison! I'm done with prison life. Anything but that."

That changed everything for Remy. She knew he had no regard for Rod's life and maybe not his own.

She stopped about three feet behind them, noting that Jasper relaxed his hold on his gun as he closed the door. She needed him to turn around.

"Now that I know your name, Jasper," she said, her voice surprisingly calm, "I have to say, you must be an awful disappointment to your parents."

Surprised, Jasper and Rod turned around to face her. That was what Remy had been hoping for. She wasn't interested in conversation, negotiation, or anything else besides freeing her husband. Before Jasper could respond, Remy shot him twice in the left knee, careful to avoid shooting near his right side where Rod was standing. At her insistence, Remy and London had taken self-defense classes several years earlier, which included learning how to shoot a multitude of firearms and where to aim.

Remy was relieved when Jasper screamed in shock and pain, then dropped his gun and fell in a heap on the floor. She was willing to shoot him again if necessary. Rod kicked the gun out of Jasper's reach and then went to his wife, removing the gun from her shaking hand.

The police rushed in with guns drawn through the front and back doors. They saw Jasper on the floor shrieking in pain and Rod holding Remy just a few feet away, his gun pointed downward. Rod didn't recognize any of them, but they knew who he and Remy were.

After retrieving both guns and allowing Remy and Rod to get properly dressed, the police walked them out through the front door. They sat in separate police cruisers where they each gave a statement to the officers on the scene and then again to Detectives Jefferson and Kinser over the phone. The entire neighborhood was out on their front lawns, taking pictures and videoing the action. At least the police had been able to keep the media out of the neighborhood.

Once the initial questioning was over, Rod and Remy were brought back together. They held each other on the small front lawn, exhausted but grateful they hadn't been hurt. They watched one ambulance take away the police officer whom Jasper had shot and another take the gunman. The paramedics were hopeful that the officer would survive but said if they had arrived just a few more minutes later, it would have been too late.

After packing up their things, Rod walked Remy to his car. They were headed to the police station, after which they would catch the next flight to Atlanta.

"I'm so proud of you, Remy," he said as they buckled in. "You must have been terrified, but you didn't hesitate, and your aim was spot on."

Remy smiled. "Thank you, baby. I would have done anything to make us safe. I wasn't aiming for his knee, though. I was aiming for his heart."

"No way! Seriously?" When she nodded, he laughed. "My God, I'm glad I was out of the way!"

"Me too!" she said, grinning.

Then they sped off, for the moment leaving everything that had happened over the past few hours behind.

17

"If everyone is moving forward together, then success takes care of itself."

Henry Ford

I WAS ON MY WAY TO DSIG. TRAFFIC WAS SURPRISINGLY LIGHT THAT morning, which was good because I was listening more intently to Remy than paying attention to the cars in front of me. Luke had set up a call with the three of us when he didn't hear back from the detectives the night before.

"Are you kidding me?" I practically screamed. "There was a mirror hidden in the wall? That's the stuff of horror movies. I can't believe you were able to stay still in there without making any noise, especially seeing everything that was going on."

"It wasn't easy," Remy replied. "When I realized he was

one of the men who ran me off the road, it took everything within me to stay calm and not try to strangle him right then and there."

"Did he say why they did it or who he worked for?"

"No. In fact, he has no idea who hired him."

"Did the detectives find anything on the first guy who was following Rod?" Luke asked.

"A little," Remy said. "He had multiple IDs on him, and it turns out he has an outstanding warrant for an assault charge. Rod got away from him just in time. Who knows what he would have tried to do."

"What about Jasper?" I asked. "He's clearly a complete psychopath."

"Jasper and his blown-off kneecap," Remy said, her voice full of pride, "are in the hospital. He lawyered up. So, right now, we don't know anything more than what we did a month ago, which is why I'm coming home. Enough of waiting the criminals out. I'm done with letting someone else dictate how I live my life."

I was so excited she was coming home!

"I agree," Luke said. "It's time for you to come home. We've arranged for a press conference with us, Rod, Jefferson, and Kinser tomorrow morning. We'll explain to the public why you went AWOL, which will comfort everyone who's grieving your loss. Jefferson and Kinser will request help from the public. I think it will resonate more when they hear your story, Remy. I don't like how we had to mislead people, but I think they'll understand."

"I hope so," Remy replied. "I'm ready to come home. I miss my life and all of you so much. I especially miss Mom. I wish she could come home too."

"You know it's not safe yet," I reminded her. We stayed silent for a second until we heard a woman on Luke's end wish him a good morning.

"Who is that?" I asked.

"It's Kelly, but that's a whole other story. Someone tried to run her off the road last night, just like they did to you, Remy."

"Kelly, as in your soon-to-be ex-wife?" Remy asked. "How's she doing? Is she alright?"

"Yeah. She wasn't hurt physically, but she was seriously shaken up. I stayed with her last night."

I was shocked. "I can't believe someone tried to hurt her. "That's terrible! This has become much more personal than trying to sabotage our business. And now poor Kelly has been drawn into this. Call me selfish, Remy, but I'm just grateful you'll be back with us. I can't wait to see you. I'm almost at the office. I called a meeting with everyone to let them know you're alive. They'll be quite surprised, but I don't want our employees to hear it on the news or social media tomorrow after the press conference. Wilson and Robert will be ecstatic. Please be sure to text us as soon as you land in Atlanta."

"I will," Remy said. "We're at the New Orleans airport now.

"Luke, let us know what happens with Kelly. She didn't sign up for any of this," I said.

"I know," he replied. "I'll investigate Kelly's situation. Both of you stay alert today. Pay attention to your surroundings. If something doesn't feel right, it probably isn't."

"Love you both," Remy said.

"I love y'all too," I replied.

"You two are my favorite sisters," Luke said. "Love you both too."

The three of us agreed to check in later that day. We all had a full morning. Remy and Rod were about to catch their flight, I was meeting with all DSIG employees, and Luke had to investigate what happened to Kelly. We needed to get going and were much happier to do it with Remy coming home.

At DSIG, Serena was looking forward to hearing about Wilson's conversation with Marge. He had seemed so ready to end things with her. She knew Marge wasn't going to take it well, but it was time for him to be honest and pull the plug. Her police training told her something was off with Marge, but it wasn't her place to get involved in their relationship. It was bad enough that she had followed him home from the office.

When I walked through the front doors of DSIG, Serena was at the front desk. She smiled. "Good morning. Lina and I have everything set up for you. A memo went out to all employees to meet in the conference room in an hour. Those working virtually will be on video. I'll dial in from here in case we have any walk-in clients."

"Thanks, Serena. I knew you and Lina would be all over it. Hey, is Wilson in yet? I was hoping to catch him before the meeting."

"No, I haven't seen him yet, but when I do, I'll let him know you're looking for him."

"Great. I'd appreciate it."

I greeted our employees who were already there and then made my way to my office. I was surprised to get a text from Luke saying he would be present for the meeting, but I was glad we could share the news together. I got a text from Wilson. It said he had COVID and wouldn't be in. It wasn't serious, just a headache and a few other symptoms. I texted him back.

Of course. Take all the time you need. Hope you feel better soon. I don't want to bother you, but there's something personal I need to share before you hear it elsewhere. If you have the strength, call me. If it's too much I understand. At the very least, listen in on the meeting if you can. And make sure Marge takes good care of you. Talk soon.

I received a thumbs-up emoji in response.

Robert knocked on my open office door. "London, I know we have a meeting coming up soon, but I wanted to check on you after that marathon deposition. How are you doing?"

"Come on in," I replied. "So much has happened since then. It seems like it was a week ago instead of just yesterday. Joey has always been the obnoxious one, but sitting across from Alexander and answering his questions was the bigger challenge for me. Thanks for navigating me through it all."

"Speaking of Alexander, why didn't you tell me about him? I would have strategized a little differently had I known. They have a lot of good junior attorneys assisting them."

"I'm sorry. I should have told you. But I don't like revisiting the past, and I figured if we prepped as we usually do, it would still serve us well. So, how did I do?"

Robert ran his fingers through his red hair as he pondered his answer. "Considering the situation, surprisingly well. You stuck with the facts and never wavered. Their client is guilty and sitting in jail, and I'd like to keep it that way. They didn't get anything from you that will change that."

I was relieved to hear his thoughts. My family had held him in high regard since he joined the company less than a year ago, just after Alexander and I broke up.

"Now it's up to the detectives to get to the bottom of this," he said.

I didn't want to blindside Robert again, so I shared the good news about Remy. Before he could reply, Luke and Kelly joined us in my office. Robert was dumbstruck for a moment, filled with disbelief.

"What? She's been alive all this time? You didn't think you could trust me with this information? I'm your attorney and your friend. If you can't confide in me then why am I here? I'm thrilled Remy is alive, but I don't know if I can work with people who don't value me or my ability to maintain confidentiality. This makes me wonder what else you've been holding back. Not just now but ever since I've been here. This isn't right! I need to get out of here before I say something I'll regret." He stormed out of the office before any of us could respond.

Luke, Kelly, and I were left there with our mouths open. Kelly's gaze passed back and forth between us. "Why didn't you tell your attorney?"

I felt unnerved. First, I hadn't told Robert about Alexander, and now Remy. I told Robert that not revealing my relationship with Alexander was about not looking to the past, but that wasn't completely true. The same went for withholding the information about Remy. There was another reason that I couldn't quite put my finger on. Luke and I looked at each other, but neither of us could answer Kelly's question.

18

"And after all, what is a lie? Tis the truth in masquerade."
Lord Byron

LUKE, KELLY, AND I ENTERED THE PACKED CONFERENCE ROOM. There were twenty chairs, and all of them were filled, with several people standing off to the side. A few other employees were on video, and others had called in. Those standing who hadn't had a chance to say hello earlier stepped up to talk to Luke and me. We shook hands and exchanged pleasantries. Kelly whispered something in Luke's ear and then stepped out of the room. I got the feeling she didn't want to be on camera.

Kelly made her way to the ladies room, then went into a stall. She had told Luke she needed some time alone to process everything. Sure, she knew she was soon to be his ex-wife, but she was familiar with so many of our employees. Paranoia had set in. She felt like they were ignoring her, and worse, that Luke was ignoring her. He knew someone had tried to run her off the road just like they had done to Remy. Even though Remy's announcement was about to be made, she wanted more attention from him. *What should I do?* She was becoming desperate, and she didn't know why. *Stop it,* she scolded herself. *You're fine. He just learned about this last night, and he hasn't left your side. He still cares.*

Kelly walked out of the stall and washed her hands. As she looked in the mirror, unbeknownst to her, she was staring at herself much like London had the day before. Kelly didn't have nearly the confidence London had, although she was beautiful in her own right. She was lean, green-eyed, and blonde, the type Luke liked. At least he used to. Although they were getting divorced, she followed him on social media and wasn't so sure anymore. His friends were a welcome mixture of just about every ethnicity she could imagine. The women he dated represented every ethnicity too, and there were plenty of them. She couldn't do anything about that, but she was focused on other things.

After leaving the restroom, she decided to go to Luke's office and dial in instead of returning to the conference room. She was just in time to hear London's voice.

"Good morning, everyone," I said with a smile, receiving many others in return. "Given the short notice of our meeting, we're glad you all could make it. That includes all of you on video and those calling in. Luke and I have some wonderful news to share. We're telling you now because we care about you and want you to hear this from us first. It's also to make sure you have accurate information before the media learns of it tomorrow."

Just get on with it, Marge thought as she listened in using

Wilson's phone. *What's this little witch about to share?*

Although Robert had stormed out of the office, he still called in to hear how the employees would respond to the news. Even the Taylor brothers and Detectives Jefferson and Kinser were on the line. Everyone was listening . . . and waiting.

The detectives were focused on employee reactions in the room, thinking some would stand out. They were ready to look at them all. The police had investigated every DSIG employee. None stood out except for Wilson's relationship with Marge. Had the detectives been monitoring the numbers of those who called in, they would have been one step closer to Marty. But, of course, Marty was prepared for that. The phone number wouldn't lead to him. None ever did.

I glanced at Luke before continuing. Although we hadn't planned it, we were both dressed in light blue jeans and black shirts. Mine was a short-sleeved bodysuit with white flowers, and his was a casual short-sleeved polo that showed a peek of his muscles. The ladies in the room couldn't help but notice.

"I know we've all been in a bit of a haze for some time now. We've had a series of attacks on our business, but much worse, we've had attacks on us personally. The police are working on these cases, and, as you know, one individual has been arrested for arson and is now in jail awaiting trial. Another was arrested for the role he played in setting his own house on fire. We're very grateful for that. We've been working with the police to identify the bigger culprit behind this. Just over four weeks ago yesterday, Remy was run off the road and left for dead at the bottom of a ravine. It was not an accident. We know someone tried to kidnap our sister. At that time the police suggested we announce that Remy was dead even though she wasn't. We did it in the hope of emboldening whoever was behind it. If they thought they "won" by taking out Remy, perhaps they would think it was time to try something similar with me or even Luke.

Those assembled emitted a collective gasp, looking around

as if Remy was going to pop out from under a chair. I let them process the revelation for a few seconds before continuing. "This was extremely difficult for all of us but especially for Remy. We knew the heartache it would cause for many of you and countless others who care about us. At the time, our family agreed with the police and thought this was the best way to draw out those who tried to hurt our family and our business. For a time, it seemed to work, and the police felt they were getting closer to solving the case. They still feel that way." I paused again, tears welling in my eyes as I thought about how close we came to losing Remy the night before. I cleared my throat. "But after another attempt to harm our family last night, it was time to stop hiding. Remy wasn't killed in that accident. She is very much alive and is on her way back to Atlanta right now. We are very excited and can't wait to welcome her back home."

As expected, reactions were mixed. Most people clapped and cheered. Others cried, and some were stunned into silence, unable to believe what they had just heard. Luke and I stayed to answer as many questions as we could. We owed it to our employees, who had been so supportive to us throughout the ordeal.

All this time Marge had thought Remy was dead. If Wilson were alive, he would have cried and cheered. Just thinking about it made her dislike the family more. Sitting in her usual spot at the kitchen table, she looked across the room at Wilson's cold body, covered in blood. "Sorry," she muttered. "Not sorry!" At that moment she knew Marty couldn't help her with Wilson. She had to figure out what to do next on her own.

When Alexander and Joey heard the news, they were speechless.

"You mean to tell me after five hours of deposing her, she kept that little treasure to herself?" Joey said. "We both interrogated her yesterday. How did we not pick up on that?"

"I told you something was off," Alexander replied. "I knew it! See? I'm a much better investigator than you!" He and Joey grinned. Being twins, they often kidded each other.

"Okay, I didn't know Remy was alive, but I knew London wasn't grieving," Alexander admitted. "Those sisters are as thick as thieves. But I'm relieved. I always liked Remy. She should be my sister-in-law, you know."

"Yeah, yeah, yeah, I know," Joey said. "But aren't you glad you're not connected to all this? Who knows where it will lead?"

"No, I'm not glad. I shouldn't be on the sidelines like some stranger. I should be at London's side. I should have been up there with her and Luke knowing and sharing this information. And our firm damn sure shouldn't be representing that piece of crap, low-level criminal, Chet Miller."

Joey looked at him in disbelief. "Snap out of it, bro. She broke up with you the night before your wedding! You may not remember it, but I was there, and I had to help pull you together after you lost it! Do you remember that?"

"Of course, I remember. I was remembering it a bit less every day, but when I saw her fine ass yesterday, I won't lie. Everything hit me again at once."

All Joey could do was shake his head.

Marty knew that Remy surviving that crash was a possibility, which was why arrangements had been made for Rod to be followed over the past two weeks. They hit the jackpot when they learned Remy was alive and being protected in Baton Rouge, and Rod led them right to her. They were so close to taking her away from that little shotgun house. It was disappointing to learn that not only had Rod *and* Remy made it out, Remy had gotten the drop on their man. Marty had underestimated her and the entire family. It was time for a change of plans. That began by revealing what Marge had so willingly shared via voicemail.

19

"Home Is a Shelter From Storms—All Sorts of Storms."
William Bennett

REMY SIGHED AND THEN TOOK A DEEP BREATH AS SHE LOOKED AROUND at the farmhouse-style home she shared with Rod. She was so grateful to be back. Back with Rod, with her family, and soon back to her life, or so she hoped. Considering all that had happened, she and Rod were fortunate to be alive. It was still hard to process it all. Thank goodness she had been able to take Jasper down before he got them. It was close, but they made it out. Remy prayed the police officer whom Jasper had shot would pull through. He had been attacked because a psychopath was after them, and it wasn't right. She knew her employees would be taken aback by the news, but she hoped they would understand why the family did it.

Luke rang Remy and Rod's doorbell. The moment Rod opened the front door, we rushed in to greet him.

"Sissy?" I called out.

"Where's my sister?" Luke said.

Remy laughed as she entered the family room to greet us, giving Luke and I a long, tight hug.

"Luke, I can't breathe," Remy said.

"My bad," he replied, releasing her. "I'm just relieved to have you here. It's been way too long."

"I know," Remy said, tears in her eyes.

"I can't believe we have our sissy back!" I said. "I'm so glad you're home." We hugged her again. Boy, had I missed my sister.

Only when the three of us separated did Remy realize that Kelly was there too.

"Kelly is that you?" she said. "It's been forever."

Kelly gave Remy a quick hug. "Sorry to tag along, but Luke and I are meeting with the police later today."

"Well, it must be a Devereaux and Jaymes thing because Rod and I are meeting with the police later too. Let's all go together."

We locked up the house, set the alarm, then made our way to the front of the house. I jumped into Rod and Remy's car, which left Luke alone with Kelly.

"Enjoy," I mouthed at Luke before shutting the car door, a smile on my face. When I saw his expression, though, I realized that wasn't exactly the outcome he was hoping for. But surely he knew I needed to spend time with Remy. My police escort followed us all. It reminded me that Remy would need a detail while these psychos were still out there.

Luke knew London meant well, but it was a thirty- or forty-minute ride depending on traffic, and it seemed to be picking up now that it was afternoon. He wasn't used to having casual conversations with Kelly anymore. Jumping in to help her with a real threat was natural for him, and he would do whatever he could to keep her safe, but he wasn't ready for this.

"So," Kelly began, "I know you're happy to have your sister back."

Luke nodded, keeping his eyes on the road. "'Happy' is an understatement. I knew where Remy was, which helped, but sometimes you don't realize how important people are in your life until they're no longer there. We couldn't call or text, and we certainly couldn't see each other. It was tough."

Kelly knew the feeling. She looked out the passenger window and sighed. When they separated, they had both agreed to the divorce, but soon she felt like she had made a mistake. At first, Luke didn't want a divorce, though he agreed something wasn't working. They tried counseling, but their marriage was clearly broken, and that brokenness created more brokenness, which was how they had ended up where they were.

Although he seemed distant, she was about to broach the topic of their relationship, suggesting that maybe they could give it another try, when a text message appeared on his CarPlay dashboard.

"Text message from Madison," Siri said. "Do you want me to read it?"

Luke reached out, meaning to clear it, but instead he hit "play" by accident. "Hey, hot stuff!" Siri said. "I left my earrings at your place the other night. How about I come by with a bottle of—"

"Stop!" Luke said, then glanced at Kelly. "Sorry." He didn't want to hurt Kelly, but their marriage was over. When he moved out, he had also moved on with his life. Now it was just a matter of formalizing it. His only plan that day was to learn more about the threat she faced. Beyond that, he was emotionally unavailable to her.

Unbelievable, Kelly thought, almost speaking the word out loud. She thought about the earrings from the night before.

She had almost bought a similar pair but thought they were too expensive. Apparently, Madison didn't mind spending the money. She would have to ask London if she knew who the woman was.

"Dirty whore," she mumbled. Thankfully, Luke had been too consumed by his thoughts to hear it.

"What's that?" he asked, glancing at her.

"Nothing. Just trying to keep my mind occupied, thinking about laundry and all the other chores I need to do at the house."

"Gotcha."

As Rod, Remy, and I followed Luke and Kelly in Remy's white four-door Tesla, Rod had to speed to keep up. I now suspected Luke was in a hurry to end his private time with Kelly.

"Have you heard anything new about Kelly's attack yet?" Rod asked.

I shook my head. "No, nothing. We're hoping the police will have something for us by the time we get to the station. I respect Jefferson and Kinser, but I suspect they know more than they're letting on. On top of that, I feel bad for Kelly. She and Luke aren't together anymore, and yet whoever is behind this included her in our turmoil. She probably hates us all now."

Rod chuckled. "Nah, I don't think so. In fact, I get the feeling she doesn't mind being a part of Luke's crazy life, even if it puts her at risk. It seems like she's trying to pick up where they left off. That reminds me, you would have been proud of your sister last night. She took control of the situation and kept her wits about her. You won't believe what she said before she shot that idiot."

I looked at Remy. "Tell me! What did you say?"

She smiled. "I don't remember. It wasn't exactly planned."

I turned back to Rod. "Well . . . ?"

"She was dead serious when she said it, and I quote, 'Jasper, you must be an awful disappointment to your parents.'

Then she shot him twice in the knee. It was like something out of a movie!"

My mouth fell open. "Oh my God, Remy. After all this is over you should teach self-defense classes! I love it!"

20

"Those who can see the strings can no longer be puppets."
Shannan Knox

THE LONGER THE FIVE OF US WAITED IN THE AGING POLICE DEPARTment lobby, the more we began to worry. Finally, I approached the receptionist.

"Hi. You said both detectives are here, right? Our appointment was thirty minutes ago."

"Yes, Ms. Devereaux," the receptionist replied. "Detectives Jefferson and Kinser are here, but there's been a new development. They'll be with you as soon as possible."

"I bet they caught a break," Luke said after I shared the news. "Maybe one of those criminals from Baton Rouge spoke up."

"That would be something," Rod replied. "Or maybe they

know who tried to run Remy and Kelly off the road. I bet—"

He stopped mid-sentence when a stranger walked in carrying a small antique clock. He looked to be in his mid-seventies and was white with a short gray beard.

A few minutes later, an older Hispanic woman came in. Her eyes swept the lobby. When she saw the man with the clock, she approached him. They spoke briefly, then he handed her the clock. Satisfied with its condition, she gave him some cash in exchange. After the woman left, he waited a full minute before he walked out, placing the money in his pocket. We all watched him go, fascinated by the exchange.

"The police advertise the lobby as a safe space to meet strangers for such exchanges," Kelly explained, as if reading our thoughts. "We're all being recorded, and the police are seconds away behind those locked doors. I've done it myself."

Before we could discuss it further, Detective Kinser walked out. "Sorry to keep you waiting, but we just learned something important. Please come on back."

As we stood up to follow him, I felt the heaviness of his words. I knew it wasn't good.

Kinser led us through the door and down a corridor. We spotted several uniformed officers and others I assumed were investigators of some kind. Most were at their desks, but others were huddled together in groups, talking. I studied their faces, hoping to get a preview of what was to come, but their expressions revealed nothing.

Kinser brought us into a small conference room. It was clear the police budget was not spent on decor. The room could barely hold eight comfortably. The table was off-white and could be broken into several smaller tables. The blue chairs were a little worn but still had a few years left in them.

As we settled in, Jefferson joined us with his laptop. The detectives looked at each other before Jefferson opened the meeting. "I'm sorry. We don't know the best way to tell you this other than to play the recording and then share what our officers found at the scene." He hit a few buttons, and then a woman's voice filled the room. Remy and I recognized Marge's shrill tone immediately. She asked someone named Marty for help. Then she said she had accidentally killed her boyfriend, Wilson, hitting him several times with a wine bottle. She rambled about him wanting to end their relationship and how he had asked her to leave. How dare he! And that's when it happened. She accidentally hit him upside the head and couldn't stop. She just lost it. Now she needed help to get rid of the body and clean up.

When the recording ended, I felt sick.

"Did you go to Wilson's house?" I asked. "You have to check! Marge is a bitter woman. Maybe she made this up." But as the words came out, I remembered getting texts from Wilson that said he was sick. The timing was too much of a coincidence.

"We have a team there now," Jefferson said. "The front door was unlocked. Marge was there and so was Wilson. I'm sorry, but everything she said was true. Wilson was found deceased with multiple abrasions to the head.

"When our officers arrived, Marge was drunk. We're letting her sober up before we talk to her. There's a lot to unpack, but we wanted to share this with you. She didn't do anything to hide what she did. We're going to ask her about Wilson but also this Marty person."

"Why would she call somebody named Marty and confess on a recording?" Remy asked through her tears. "It makes no sense."

"We think Marge and Marty have something to do with what's happening to all of you. She trusted him with her entire story and thought he could or would help. The question is, why and what else does Marty know?"

We were all devastated. I knew Marge was mean-spirited and had always thought Wilson could do better, but I never expected anything like this. It was unbelievable. Now Wilson was dead. He had been a loyal employee, someone we relied upon, but more importantly, he had been a good person. It cut me to the core.

"How did you get this recording?" Luke asked.

"I don't think that matters," Kelly said. We all turned and looked at her in surprise. "The point is they got it," she continued. "Now they can hold Marge responsible for what she's done. Isn't that what's most important?" Kelly had a habit of saying awkward things at times. That was one of the things that was off-putting to Luke.

"Yes it is," Kinser replied. "But we received this recording for a reason. We need to know what that reason is and who wants us to know about it."

"Again, we're sorry for your loss," Jefferson said, "but we asked you to come down here so we could talk to you about a few other things. We've been talking to Johnny Lott and his court-appointed attorney. He's a low-level player in this. As you know, he's being charged with setting his own house on fire, but we're confident he doesn't know anything else. He's pleading guilty and will testify against Chet Miller, who we believe got his marching orders from Marge."

"Things are coming together," Kinser added. "We know things aren't moving as fast as you would like, but we're still moving forward."

Jefferson turned to Kelly. "We need to ask you more about your accident. It sounds similar to Remy's, but there are a lot of differences. How about we go into another room and talk through what happened step by step?"

"I'll be happy to, but it happened so fast," Kelly replied. "I don't know if I can share more than I already have."

"Oh, you'd be surprised how much the mind recalls once you walk back through it step by step," Jefferson said as he stood up.

"Can Luke join us?" Kelly asked as she also stood.

"It will be better for you if he doesn't," Jefferson said. We were already unnerved due to Wilson's death, but this exchange caught everyone's attention.

"Detective, is there something else we should know?" Luke asked.

"No, it's common practice," Kinser replied. "Trust me, Luke, you'd only be a distraction. Kelly will be just fine with Jefferson."

The rest of us were okay with that, but Kelly didn't seem to be on board.

"Okay, Detective, you know what's best," Luke said. "Kelly, I'll be here when you're done."

She looked at Luke as if she were hoping he would say more. When he didn't, she left with Jefferson.

After the two of them left the conference room, the rest of us decided we needed time to digest what we had just learned about Wilson. Kinser let us through a side door into a courtyard for some fresh air, then left us alone for fifteen minutes.

Remy, Luke, Rod, and I didn't say anything. Rod hugged Remy. I sat down with my head on Luke's shoulder, wiping my eyes with some tissues I picked up in the conference room.

When our meeting resumed, Kinser was gentle with us. "I know this is tough, but we have some positive news from Baton Rouge."

"Well, we sure could use some," Rod replied.

"The police officer who was guarding Remy just came out of surgery and will recover. Luckily, his injuries weren't life-threatening."

"Oh, thank goodness," Remy whispered. We all needed to hear that, especially after learning about Wilson.

"Jasper, the man you shot, was in a talkative mood this morning after knee surgery. Our people met him at the hospital, and it seems like he's trying to get some kind of deal, although it's way too early to consider that. He said his contact had a distorted male voice, but other times it sounded like a woman. After Wilson's death, we suspect the woman may have been Marge. We hope she's able to talk to us soon. Jasper also indicated other men had been looking for Remy too. They were all under instructions to follow Rod in the hopes of finding Remy. He emphasized that they weren't supposed to kill anybody. As you thought, Remy, he was hired to kidnap you, but, if necessary, they were authorized to use force."

We all took a deep breath. I already suspected it, but to hear it from Kinser confirmed it.

"Think about it," Kinser continued. "This began with somebody targeting your business with multiple arsons. It became more personal with Remy's hit-and-run, and attempt to kidnap her or worse." He looked at Luke. "The next attack was on your wife, Kelly, though not nearly as severe." Then he locked eyes with me. "We believe the next attack will be on you, London. But by now they've learned from their mistakes. This time will be much more organized and targeted."

None of us were shocked. After Remy's attack, we were expecting it. But when everyone looked at me, I finally lost it.

21

"One cannot be betrayed if one has no people."
The Usual Suspects

"KELLY, THANKS FOR AGREEING TO MEET WITH ME," JEFFERSON SAID. "I know these kinds of interviews can be difficult. I'm here to get to the bottom of this for the family's sake. I've been working closely with them and have grown quite fond of them." Kelly noticed he didn't include her as part of the family.

"Of course. I want to get to the bottom of this too and will help as much as I can," she said. "I love every one of them. Regardless of what's going on, we're all very close. Despite our separation, Luke and I still care for each other. I'm not sure if you know, but London introduced us. She and I have been friends since college."

"Yes, I'm aware you were friends with London first. Did you become friends with Remy too?"

"Oh, absolutely. I went home with London lots of times in New Orleans. I enjoyed spending time with the Devereaux family. Their parents were such good people. They welcomed me every time I walked through the door. I was there when their father passed away. It's good to see their mom still living a full life, especially after losing Mr. Devereaux over ten years ago."

"Right. Well, thanks for being so willing to share, Kelly. I don't mind telling you that this case has been challenging. We're not sure if one sibling is more of a target than the others or if it's a matter of sending a message by hitting the entire family. That's why I'm curious about your accident and how it relates to them. Can you elaborate again on what happened?"

"Sure. As you already know, I was driving home on Dwyer Road, the street that leads to my subdivision. It's a two-lane road, and there are several areas where it's curvy and, if you're not careful, you can run off the road and into a deep ravine. I pay close attention every time I drive it. The speed limit is thirty-five miles per hour, though I was probably driving a little faster than that when a truck came up behind me and hit my rear bumper.

"I was shocked, especially considering I was probably driving about ten miles over the speed limit. No cars were in the other lane, so whoever it was could have passed me. Instead, they hit me from behind not once but twice. It was terrifying.

"The first time, I tapped my brakes, thinking it was an accident, and was planning to stop at a nearby pullout. I slowed down and turned my four-way flashers on. The next thing I knew, they hit me again, harder this time, and my car spun right around. That's when I realized they had done it on purpose.

"When my car stopped spinning, I was in the other lane facing the opposite direction. By that time cars were approaching from both directions. Fortunately, people stopped to help, and the truck that had hit me drove off. I called the police and then I called Luke."

"Did you get a look at the driver?" Jefferson asked.

"He was a white male with short brown hair. He looked young, but other than that I couldn't say much more. I was too terrified."

"You said it was a truck. What make and color?"

"Well, I'm not a big car person. But it was a two-door silver or gray truck. I know it had an open bed."

"Okay. Do you think you could recognize the driver if you saw him again?"

"I think so. I'd be happy to look at any pictures you have."

"I appreciate that. The other attacks have been more severe. Why do you think the driver didn't pursue you even more after you spun out?"

"This is getting repetitive. I'm not sure how to answer that since I already did. I don't think like these criminals, Detective. Again, other drivers were on the road by then. I suppose he knew it was time to disappear."

"Of course. I just meant that it seems like you were very fortunate to get away unscathed."

Kelly raised her eyebrow but didn't respond.

"What made you call Luke? You two have been separated for some time, haven't you?"

"What can I say? Old habits die hard. It was almost ten o'clock at night. I was shaken up, and separated or not, Luke is still my husband, so I knew he would come. Are there any more questions, detective? I get the feeling you're holding something back."

Jefferson forced a smile. "Since you asked, I'm going to be straightforward with you, Kelly. I believe you when you say you were hit from behind multiple times. I know you were spun around, and I don't doubt you were terrified. But I also think it was completely unrelated to what's going on with the family."

"Then what was it about?"

"I believe the incident was a cry for attention. I think you set it up. You paid some teenager to hit you to make it seem like someone was coming after you. But you just wanted Luke to believe that, so he would come to your rescue. Isn't that right?"

Kelly scoffed. "Oh, please! You're reading way too much into things. Like I said, it made sense to call Luke, but I didn't arrange an accident—risk my life on a curvy road with a steep drop—just to get back together with him. If I want that to happen, there are other means, Detective. Surely, as a man, you know that."

Ignoring her last statement, his face turned serious. "Are you going to tell them, or should I? They have real threats to contend with, and they don't need to be distracted by this foolishness."

Kelly became surprisingly calm. Having told the first lie, it was easy to tell another. "You're not listening, Detective. I'm a lot of things, but I'm not desperate. I have my own family and plenty of friends, and trust me, lots of men are interested in dating me. I don't need to play the damsel in distress to keep Luke or any of the Devereauxs in my life. Instead of accusing me of these absurdities, your officers should be investigating this terrible act of aggression against me. I could have been hurt or worse."

"We agree on one thing, Kelly," Jefferson replied, the look in his eyes intensifying, "we should be investigating this. We have excellent officers who work in our accident investigations unit. I knew they were good, but I didn't know they would be able to unravel your case in less than twenty-four hours. It's amazing what city cameras capture these days."

Kelly didn't realize there were cameras on the road to her subdivision. That was one of the reasons why she had picked the location.

"The good news is, we have the entire accident on video. You were very factual in the details of what took place. As for the truck, it's a blue Ram 1500. The license plate was missing, but we've already put out a BOLO—be on the lookout—for that truck. Something tells me it won't be difficult to find, considering it has front-end damage."

Just then Jefferson received a text. He looked at his phone and then smirked. "It's amazing how fast these BOLOs work. Look at these two pictures, and you'll see what I mean."

He handed her his phone. The first picture looked like the truck that hit her, although she wasn't sure. When she scrolled to the second picture, she saw a mugshot of the eighteen-year-old she had hired. Thankfully, she had never met him, having arranged things through a third party. She was surprised at how easy it was to get so many things on the black market in Atlanta, but she would never forget the driver's terrible acne from the prior picture she had been shown. She looked up at Jefferson. "Is this the guy who nearly ran me off the road?"

"I think you know the answer to that, Kelly, considering you paid him a thousand dollars to do it."

The blood drained from her face, realizing she'd been caught. "I've had enough!" Kelly said, slamming her hand on the table. "You can't prove this because it didn't happen that way. That kid may have been paid by someone, but it wasn't me. I was attacked, and I have no idea if it's connected to what's happening to Luke and his family or not. I never claimed that it was. But I certainly don't appreciate you accusing me of a crime. You better be ready to prove that accusation if you choose to repeat it. And when it comes to Luke, I suggest you stay out of my way!"

She was about to leave when they heard yelling from the other conference room.

"We'll resume this later," Jefferson said as he hurried out, Kelly right behind him.

22

"There comes a point in your life when you need to stop reading other people's books and write your own."

Albert Einstein

IT WAS TOO MUCH. I STOOD UP AND STARTED SHOUTING. "YOU SHOULD know why this is happening! If you and Jefferson and this entire department had done your jobs, you would have caught the people behind this, and poor Wilson would still be alive. But no. You've done almost nothing! Nothing! You're supposed to protect us, but you haven't. If it weren't for Remy shooting that psycho, she and Rod would be dead too! Now I'm next! What good are any of you?"

Two officers heard my rant and ran into the conference room, followed by Jefferson and Kelly. Detective Kinser gave them the all-clear sign, and the officers backed out. I glared at them and Kinser, daring them to approach me. Remy, Rod, and Luke nodded in response to my outburst to confirm our solidarity.

Kinser waited for us to settle down before continuing. "I get it. I'm as frustrated as you are. We're working hard to catch these people. Jefferson and I care about all of you. Our priority is your safety and to end this. Don't doubt that."

I sat down again. Luke put his arm around my shoulders. "We know," he said. "It's just never-ending. Now you're telling us London is the next target. What do you suggest we do, considering this new threat?"

"We've been thinking about that. None of us like the way things went down in Baton Rouge. This time we think having two officers *inside* the house with London makes more sense. If there isn't any visible protection on the outside, whoever is after you might be more likely to try something."

"Whatever. I don't care," I replied. "All I know is I'll be waiting with a shotgun to take care of business because it's clear the only ones capable of doing that are us."

Both detectives grimaced, partly because it hurt but also because there was some truth to it. Whoever was heading this up always seemed to be a step ahead of us.

As Jefferson and Kinser went on to talk about logistics, we all agreed that two officers would be posted to my place that evening. Another officer would be assigned to Rod and Remy, and one more would be with Luke and Kelly. Luke felt compelled to stay with Kelly for at least another night even though the detectives minimized the connection between her incident and the case. The detectives and a patrol unit would drive around our houses later during the night, but they wouldn't post any officers outside. Once we got through the night, we would hold a press conference in the morning to reveal Remy's circumstances with the community.

Luke and Rod talked amongst themselves and then asked the detectives to leave the room for a few minutes. They knew there were cameras and mics in the room, but secrecy wasn't the point. They just wanted to check on all of us to confirm we were solid with the plan.

"I'm okay," I said once we were alone. "I just had to get all that off my chest. Who knows what will happen next? Maybe nothing for a while, but we have to take charge of our well-being. What do you think about all of us staying at the same place tonight?"

Everybody chewed on that for a few seconds, then Rod nodded in agreement. "I like that." I smiled, thinking he was joking. "I'm serious, London," he said. "Remy and I survived last night because we were together. If she had been alone, I don't think she would have made it."

"It's true," Remy agreed. "I like the idea too. We can all stay at our house and decide where we go from there tomorrow."

Luke shook his head. "I don't know. Won't that make us an easier target?"

"We can have an old-fashioned slumber party," Kelly said, smiling.

"This isn't a party, Kelly," Luke said, his frustration showing. She fell silent. Regardless, I'm sure she was happy to have Luke for another night.

Once the detectives agreed to the arrangement—they insisted we stay at my place instead of Rod and Remy's, seeing as they assumed I would be the next target—we left the police station in the same cars we arrived in.

"Wilson is dead," Remy said as we pulled onto the highway. "How could Marge kill him?"

"I know," I replied. "We just shared the good news about you with our employees. Now we have to tell them this. I don't know how to do that. My heart is broken for his family. I'll reach out to them tomorrow and offer our condolences. I'll also ask them to share the funeral arrangements once they decide on them. I'm sure a lot of people from DSIG will want to go."

"Sorry to say it, but it'll probably be on the news before

you manage to share it," Rod said.

I nodded in agreement. "Good point. I'll call Lina and ask her to set up a call with us, Robert, Serena, and the supervisors. After that, they can gather their employees together in small groups to break the news."

Luke and Kelly were a few cars behind. Kelly was worried. She decided she should go on the offense regarding her accident. "The police don't think my hit-and-run was related to the other incidents. Jefferson went so far as to suggest I planned the whole thing. How insulting is that?"

Luke looked at her in surprise. "Why does he think that?"

"Because he's incompetent. But besides that, he thinks since I'm not dead or practically dead, it can't be related. They found the guy who did it. He said he was paid a thousand dollars to attack me, and they think I gave him the money! It's the craziest thing I've ever heard in my life!"

"They identified the guy already? That's impressive considering how slowly everything else was going until yesterday. Don't worry. I'll talk to them. It's downright unthinkable to imply you were involved in your own hit-and-run." They stopped at a red light, and he looked over at her and smiled. "Don't worry, Kelly. They'll find whoever paid him to attack you. You're a lot of things, but you're no liar, and you're certainly no criminal. I'll make sure they know that and focus on the actual people behind this."

"Thank you, Luke," she replied, smiling in return. "That would be great. And I'm glad you know that."

Kelly looked out the window again. She hadn't thought things out very well. If the police unraveled most of what had happened in the past twenty-four hours, it wouldn't take them long to prove she arranged it. She was worried about the investigation and how Luke would react to it all once he learned she really was a liar and a criminal.

23

"Unity without verity is no better than conspiracy."
Author Unknown

It was still early Friday afternoon when Rod pulled up to my house. Remy and I were in the midst of the call with DSIG leadership regarding Wilson. It was a difficult conversation. Rod got out to give us some privacy.

As we talked, the two police officers assigned to us pulled up, one female and one male. Jefferson and Kinser hand-picked them for the assignment.

When Remy and I finally got out of Rod's car, both of us were teary-eyed.

"That was horrible," Remy said. "Serena took it harder than I expected. I didn't realize she was with him just before he was attacked. Even though there was nothing she could have done, this will weigh on her for a long time."

"I know," I said. "I just hope she takes some time off to recover from all of this."

The police were in plain clothes, but both were wearing their duty belts. They introduced themselves as Bobby Waters and Sonya Perry and said wherever I went, they would follow. They also reminded us that patrols would be made outside the house and at Remy and Luke's. Although the police thought I was the next target, they had no idea when the criminals would strike. I hoped I didn't require police protection forever.

I turned to the female officer. "Well, Sonya, I really need to release some of this stress. Are you up for joining me at the gym? I could use a workout."

"That's fine," she replied. "We'll check out the house first. Once we confirm it's all clear, I'll go with you. Bobby can stay here."

Rod and Remy agreed to return that evening to spend the night, then went home to get their things. Luke and Kelly did the same.

Sonya and I went to the gym and had a great workout. For a good two hours, I was able to forget the attacks on my family and business. I was even able to push Wilson's death out of my mind temporarily.

Once we got back to the house, the officers stayed out of my way while I went into my home office to deal with a few work-related items.

The doorbell rang at around 6:00 p.m. It was Luke and Kelly, overnight bags in hand.

"Hey, sis, where are we sleeping, and what do you have to eat?" Luke asked. "I'm starving."

"You can have any of the guest rooms upstairs. I'm pretty sure Rod and Remy will claim the downstairs bedroom since it's the biggest. I thought we could just order something once everybody gets here." I had four guest rooms, so they had plenty of room to spread out, though Kelly and Luke would have to share a Jack-and-Jill bathroom. Kelly seemed to be okay with that, though I wasn't so sure about Luke.

A few minutes later, the three of us convened at the kitchen table. "I remember the night you met Alexander. It was at Christian Allen's pool party," Kelly said out of the blue.

"Now that's a blast from the past," I replied. "He was with Joey that night. You know, Christian is still one of my best friends. My other bestie, Suzette Means, was the one who introduced us."

"That's right! I remember Joey being there too. I kept confusing him with Alexander. How did you not get them mixed up?"

"It's something about the eyes. When we met, they were both very engaging and smart, not to mention good-looking."

"Good looking? They're total hotties!" Kelly laughed, then glanced at her soon-to-be ex-husband. "But only second to Luke!"

He ignored the comment, focused on his phone, and I tried not to roll my eyes. "Yeah, they're pretty hot. Anyway, when Alexander looked at me, his eyes were warm and soft, and there was a spark that I caught right away. Joey's eyes aren't like that. Call me crazy, but they seem cold and darker. I picked up on it that first day."

"That is weird! I never noticed it. I'll pay more attention the next time I see them, if ever. I remember both of them were interested in you, though."

"I know. The three of us never talked about it after Alexander and I started dating, but it was never an issue. Once we went on a few dates, Xander and I knew we were meant to be together."

Kelly glanced at Luke, who was only half listening as he texted someone. Kelly couldn't help but notice the smile on his face. It was the kind of smile she had elicited from him just a few years ago, but no longer. She imagined ripping his phone out of his hand and texting whatever slut was on the other end that he was getting back with his wonderful wife and to forget he ever existed!

About twenty minutes later, Rod and Remy arrived with groceries. To everyone's delight, rather than order out, Rod had decided to treat us to his culinary skills. As he headed toward the kitchen which opened to the family room, Remy brought their overnight bags to the first-floor guestroom. Everyone was glad to hear Rod was cooking and even happier when we saw him pull out the holy trinity of Creole cuisine—onions, bell peppers, and celery. We knew whatever he was cooking would be delicious.

Shortly after Rod started chopping, the doorbell rang again. Officer Waters answered it. It was Serena, a distraught look on her face. She and Waters had worked together at the Atlanta PD. She had left on good terms and had a good reputation. They spoke for a few minutes before she came in.

When Serena saw Rod, Remy, Luke, Kelly, and the other officer with me, she put her hand to her chest. "I'm sorry. I didn't realize you had a full house. I was just so upset about Wilson that I didn't want to be alone."

"I'm glad you came," I said. "There's no point in you staying home alone at a time like this. How about I open some wine? Then we can toast Wilson."

Everyone agreed, so I opened a few bottles of red wine and let them breathe for a few minutes before pouring for everyone except the two officers, who had water and coffee instead. I was about to make a toast when the doorbell rang again.

It was Robert. Like Serena, he was surprised to see so many people at my house. "Sorry to interrupt," he said. "I couldn't make today's call, but I heard about Wilson. It's just awful. London and Remy, I'm sure we can talk next week. Now doesn't seem to be a good time."

He turned to go, but Remy grabbed his arm. "Robert, you don't have to be so lawyer-like all the time. Come in and have a drink with us. We could all use one."

He thanked her for the offer and then rejoined the group, though he looked like he had something he wanted to get off his chest. "Um . . . I overreacted earlier today. I was caught off guard when I realized I didn't know everything that was going on, especially about you, Remy. And Alexander."

"It's okay, Robert," I replied. "I understand completely. I should have shared both pieces of information with you. I trust you and want you to stay with DSIG." I smiled and opened my arms for a hug. Forgive me?"

He stepped into the hug without hesitation. "Of course. And there's really nothing to forgive. Yes, I'll stay on. Where else would I go?"

We finally made a toast to Wilson, which included our hope that he was in a better place. "To Wilson!" we said in unison as we clinked our glasses.

Despite the reason we were together, everyone was becoming more lighthearted. We had Remy back. Rod's delicious-smelling dinner was almost ready, and the wine was flowing. Rod and I set up the food on the kitchen island in a buffet style so everyone could help themselves to his seafood jambalaya, short ribs, spinach salad, and warm French bread. If we had room for dessert, Blue Bell vanilla ice cream with pralines and bourbon sauce was waiting for us.

Robert was in the midst of loading his plate when he paused. "I think I know why you're being targeted and who's behind it," he said. That caught everyone's attention.

"Okay, then lay it out for us," Luke said. "You've got the floor."

"It's Alexander Taylor," Robert replied, his voice slightly elevated. "And I would have figured that out sooner if London had been upfront with me about her relationship with him."

So much for the apology, I thought. This was what two generous pours of wine brought out. Robert's face was red, his expression a cross between hurt and anger. *I wished he brought his wife along to keep him in line.*

"Dude, first watch how you talk to my sister. Second, if

you don't, I'll kick your ass right out of here. You feel me?"

"I didn't mean it the way it came out," Robert said.

"Yes, you did," I replied, my voice calm. "Just say what you have to say."

"Again, I'm sorry, London. It's just that—"

"You have five seconds to make your point," Luke said, standing.

"Okay! It's one of the simplest reasons in the world. Revenge. Alexander was blindsided and heartbroken by the breakup the night before the wedding. I'm sorry, London, but you really should have nipped that in the bud well before then. A little selfish, don't you think?"

I had to look away, knowing it was true.

"You were his world, and in one night you took it all away from him," Robert continued. "Think about it. I didn't even know about your relationship when I met him at the deposition. But I knew something was up as soon as I saw the way he reacted to you. That man is still in love with you."

The room went quiet as everyone considered Robert's theory.

"Let me get this straight," Luke said. "You think this stand-up guy who happens to be a successful attorney would commit arson and attempt murder just to get back at his ex-fiancée?"

Robert nodded. "I do."

"Man, how much have you had to drink?" Rod asked. "You don't know Alexander, but the rest of us do. There's no way he's behind this."

"I'm almost positive it's him."

"The detectives have investigated almost everyone we know," Luke said. "Have you shared your theory with them?"

"Not yet. But I will."

"Then get ready to be sued for slander and a whole lot more!" a voice boomed from the foyer.

Everyone turned at once and saw Alexander standing with my mother.

24

"Make sure the lions you roll with aren't snakes in disguise."
Sophocles

MARGE WOKE UP WITH A MAJOR HEADACHE AND SERIOUS COTTON mouth, her stringy brown hair matted to the left side of her face. She looked around, not recognizing her surroundings. Then she saw the bars, and it hit her.

"Wilson!" she yelled. "Oh my God, Wilson!"

A female officer approached her cell. "I see somebody's finally up. I'll let the detectives know you're awake."

"Wait," Marge said as the officer turned away. "Can you tell me if Wilson is . . . you know, okay?" The officer looked at her in disbelief. Marge had struck him in the head repeatedly with a wine bottle and then choked him, leaving him to lie in a pool of his own blood for hours without rendering aid. How could she think he was still alive? "Please, I need to know," Marge said.

"I'm not sure, but I bet the detectives will know," the officer replied.

"Alright. Make sure they come here as soon as possible. I need to know about my sweet Wilson."

Thirty minutes later, Marge was transferred to an interrogation room. When Jefferson and Kinser walked in, she gave them a hopeful look.

"Hello, Marge. I'm Detective Jefferson, and this is my partner, Detective Kinser. I think you know why we're here."

As Jefferson sat down, he noticed that Marge looked hungover. The room was small enough that he could smell the alcohol on her breath.

"How is Wilson? I need to know how he's doing. If you tell me that, I'll tell you whatever you want to know."

"That's good to hear, Marge," Kinser replied. "You hurt Wilson pretty badly. You might recall, we had to take him away in an ambulance. We'll check on him after we talk. How's that?"

"Thank you. I appreciate it."

Jefferson realized she wasn't thinking clearly if she thought Wilson had survived the attack.

"Marge, we have several questions for you," he began. "We heard your message asking for help after you attacked Wilson. Why don't you tell us who you called and why? We want to know every detail and what this has to do with the Devereaux family."

Marge snorted. "Fine. I'll tell you, but I'm not a fan of those Devereaux people."

"We figured that. Start from the beginning, and tell us everything you know. Don't make it worse on yourself by lying to us."

After asking for some water, Marge shared how she didn't care much for London or Remy because they refused to recommend her construction company to their clients. "They have so many customers with damage to their homes. Did you know they have a list of contractors they recommend for repairs? But they refuse to add my company to it. They claim it would be a conflict of interest because of my relationship with Wilson. That's a bunch of bull. My business wasn't doing well, and they knew it. I know London was ultimately behind the decision, but Remy was probably in on it too."

The detectives nodded, encouraging her to continue. "One day I got a call from a man who claimed he knew about my financial predicament and wanted to help me. He knew my business was struggling, and he agreed it was awful and selfish of the Devereaux sisters not to lend a hand, especially since they relied on Wilson for so much.

"He seemed to know a lot about my situation, but at first I blew him off. I didn't know this person. It could have been anybody. Heck, it could have been their brother just testing me. I have to say, as much as I don't like the family, I'd make an exception for him. That man looks like he knows what to do with a big girl like me."

"Marge, try to stay on track," Jefferson said.

She smiled. "I'm just saying. But fine. After the second call, I was curious and asked what he wanted from me. Apparently, he wanted revenge on the Devereauxs for something they did, and he needed my help, while helping me at the same time. His problems with that family sounded pretty personal."

"Did he say what he wanted from you specifically?" Jefferson asked.

"Well, simply put, he laid out a plot to hit them in their pocketbook. He wanted to commit arson against their business. You know, find customers who were willing to set fires to the houses DSIG insured. He would pay me to execute the plan. It was supposed to be just one at first. I'm no dummy, so I told him before I would consider doing anything, he had to prove he was legit. The next thing I knew, I had five thousand dollars in cash waiting for me at the house the next day. That's when I knew he was serious. The package included a phone number. I called and left a voicemail. He returned my call that same day.

"We talked about me hiring someone to set the fire. He gave me several addresses and told me to pick one. I hired my delinquent nephew, Chet, who solicited his friend, Johnny. He actually wanted to burn his own house down for a profit. It was perfect because he was already insured with them. That made it easy. Marty, as I started calling my new partner, gave me another ten thousand dollars once it was done. I gave Chet half of it and then kept the rest. His friend Johnny wanted to do it, so he didn't get paid anything. He thought he'd get a big windfall, but, of course, he was wrong.

"That was just the beginning. Once we set that fire, Marty wanted more. He said the one loss didn't mean anything to DSIG or the Devereauxs. He needed us to commit more arsons. We started six fires in total. Marty wanted the family's attention and, unfortunately for us, we got it."

"Did you ever meet this, Marty?" Kinser asked.

Marge shook her head. "No."

"Would you recognize his voice if you heard it again?"

"I'm not sure. The truth is, a male called me at first. Then after that, they used a voice changer to disguise the voice. Sometimes it sounded like a different male, but other times it sounded like a woman. I'm not positive who I was working with.

"Before long, Marty told me that even though there were multiple arsons, it wasn't hitting them the way he anticipated. DSIG started investigating the fires and denied payments for them. It wasn't enough because they weren't impacted financially the way he planned. Now Marty was out sixty-five thousand dollars because he had paid me ten thousand for each fire plus the advance. He must have some money because he didn't seem to care about that.

"He didn't share much with me, but he got agitated easily. He wanted to make the attacks more personal. I have some acquaintances who aren't the most stand-up fellas. So, I told him I could hire someone to commit a hit-and-run, though for a higher fee. Marty agreed to pay double for someone to do it. The intent wasn't to kill anyone, but he was interested in a kidnapping. My contact was a man named Jasper. One day while the sisters were out investigating the fire scenes, they split up. That's when Jasper did it. We all thought Remy was dead. They even had a funeral for her.

"At some point, Marty had a weird feeling she was alive, so he had Jasper follow Remy's husband around just in case. I thought Remy was dead for sure until London and Luke made their announcement. But here's the thing: Marty wasn't after Remy. Jasper and his partner made a mistake. London was the target. Marty wasn't happy when he heard the wrong woman went down that ravine. And if I've learned anything from our brief conversations, Marty won't stop until he has London exactly where he wants her, which could mean in a grave."

"What do you think Marty has planned next?" Kinser asked.

"I don't know. That snake cut his ties with me. I was useful until I wasn't. I was so stupid to let my feelings get in the way of my common sense. He played me." She looked down at her lap. "Over and over again, he played me." She looked up at the detectives again. "Tell me, was it Marty who sent that recording to you?"

"To be honest, we're not sure who sent it," Kinser said.

Marge looked down again, as if realizing for the first time, there were serious ramifications for her actions. "That's really all I know. Are you arresting me?"

"Yes," Jefferson replied. "The district attorney will decide what the charges will be, but we're recommending multiple charges, including arson, aggravated assault, assault and battery, conspiracy, and manslaughter. There could be more."

Marge looked up at them in horror. "No, no, no! I was tricked into this. None of this is my fault! How could I have known what Marty was really up to?"

"Oh, I think you knew plenty," Jefferson said. "You were

all in Marge. You despise this family and were thrilled to find a partner in crime. These are serious charges. You may want to find a good attorney. And Marge, you need to know something: right now, there is no evidence of this Marty. There are no financial deposits and no calls we can trace. You're the only person tied to Chet and Johnny. Earlier today, Jasper talked. He didn't name you, but said he spoke to a female. I bet if he hears your voice, he'll recognize it. They didn't get orders from anyone else. It was all you. If Marty exists, I suggest you show us some proof. You can help yourself by telling us what's in store for London."

"Believe me, Marty is real, but like I told you, he cut me loose. I don't know about anything else."

The detectives nodded at each other and then got up to leave, signaling for an officer to come back in and get Marge.

"Wait just a minute!" she cried. "I'll find the proof somehow. But how can I be charged with manslaughter? Remy is alive and well. I listened in on that call and heard it straight out of London's nasty mouth."

"Oh, it's not Remy who's dead," Kinser said. "It's Wilson. You killed him, and for that, you'll have to pay the price."

Marge crumpled in her seat. Her world was ending, and Marty had just washed his hands of her.

25

"The universe doesn't answer questions. It simply gives you signs."
Lukas Boyer

Remy and I looked at each other, then back at the two people we never thought we'd see that night. "Mom? Xander? What are you doing here? And together at that?" I took a deep breath as I saw Xander *and* Officer Waters, who had opened the door when he recognized Mom.

Luke got to them first and gave Mom a big hug and a kiss on the cheek. Remy and I followed suit. Our mother looked gorgeous, as usual, in a vibrant multicolored summer dress and gold sandals. Her gold jewelry accented her honey-colored hair. She was a vision of me thirty years in the future.

Luke and Alexander gave each other a bro handshake

hug.

"Alexander, I haven't seen you in forever!" Remy said as she stood on her tiptoes and hugged him. "We're happy to see you, Mom, but we all thought you were still in San Diego!"

"I was," my mother replied, "but when London told me you were coming back, I knew it was time to come home too. There's no need for me to be separated from my children. We've always stayed in touch, so when I flew in today, I called my son-in-love to pick me up from the airport."

I jumped on that, turning my back to Alexander, "Seriously Mom, he's not your son-in-love," I hissed.

"And he's standing right here," Alexander replied.

I turned to look at him. "I know you are. I'm just trying to figure out why."

"Unless you marry someone else, London, he'll always be my son-in-love," Mom said. "Speaking of sons-in-love, I know that wonderful smell can only be coming from something Rod created."

Mom walked into the family room where Rod and Kelly greeted her. Luke and Remy introduced her to the others.

I pulled Alexander into my office, which was just off the foyer. "What are you doing here? I know you brought Mom, and Officer Waters let you in, but do you really still have a key?"

Alexander smiled and pulled out his key ring, which included my front door key. "Oh, you mean this?" he teased, shaking the keys just out of my reach.

I tried to grab them, but he pulled back. I looked up at his handsome face. "What are you, twelve? I'm not playing games with you, Xander!"

"Beautiful, feisty London. I love playing games with you. But I have some business to take care of first with that so-called attorney of yours. I didn't like something about him when we met, and I especially don't like him now. He straight up accused me of tormenting you and your family. I would never do that."

"I know. I can't believe he said that. Let's go talk to him."

"There you two are." Mom said as we entered the living room. "Is the wedding back on?"

Remy almost spit out her wine in laughter.

"Mom, please. Just stop," I said. Our mother had always loved Alexander, and that wasn't going to change.

"You really should have talked to us before you flew down here," Luke said. "There's so much going on. It's not safe yet."

"I knew you'd feel that way," Mom replied. "That's why I told Alexander instead of any of you." Our hands were tied. She was back in town, and that was that.

Alexander didn't want to offend my mom, but he couldn't hold back against Robert either. He got into his personal space, his arms crossed. "You were saying?"

Robert backed up, his hands raised. "I think I've worn out my welcome. Alexander, I don't know you that well, so I'm not here to say what you did or didn't do. I'm just saying it's obvious to me that you have a reason to want to hurt this family—London in particular. You can at least admit that."

Xander scoffed. "Unbelievable. You're right about one thing though. You *don't* know me. If you did, you'd know how I feel about the people in this house. You'd also know I would be the last person to want to hurt them. You don't know jack about me, so don't go running your mouth about something you know nothing about. Otherwise, I'll make you pay in more ways than you can imagine."

Robert's hackles rose. "Are you threatening me?"

"No, man, I'm not threatening you. I'm *telling* you. Know for a fact that I will tear you apart in every way possible. I'll take your property, your money, your future, your life, as you know it. You won't be the same man after I finish with you. Now, this isn't my house, but I do believe I speak for everyone here when I say leave, and don't come back. Not now and not ever!"

The house went silent. Even the police officers were quiet. Robert had messed up in a lot of ways, and he knew it. He tried to make his way toward me, but Alexander blocked him. Finally, Robert surrendered. "Hey, it's all good. I'm good. London, I just want to say I'm sorry yet again. Can I please talk to you tomorrow and try to explain everything?"

"No, Robert. We're done. Human resources will be in touch with you to discuss your departure from DSIG. We don't have anything else to say."

With that, Waters escorted Robert toward the door while everyone else watched. Before he went out, Robert turned back. "You know, London, you could have made a completely different choice. Things didn't have to go this way."

"Get him out of here!" Luke yelled. Waters practically slammed the door in Robert's face.

We were all stunned. I was also disappointed.

"Unbelievable," Serena said. "I never would have thought Robert was like that in a million years. He's always been so mild-mannered. This makes me question everything." She paused. "Now that he's gone, though, maybe I should leave too."

"Serena, you came here because you didn't want to be alone. Has that changed?" Remy asked. Serena shook her head. "Then you're welcome to stay as long as you want. Right, London?"

"Right!" I replied.

Surprisingly, it didn't take long for us to switch gears and resume eating, as if Robert had never been there.

"Man, I forgot how good your cooking is, Rod," Alexander said. "Now I have to get back into this family for real." He shot a glance at me, but I wasn't smiling.

While Mom filled everyone in on our cousins in San Diego, Alexander's cell phone buzzed in his pocket. It was Joey asking if they were still on for later that night. When London's mother called him to pick her up from the airport, he had completely forgotten that Joey wanted to meet up at a new club in Atlanta. Alexander texted him back, telling him to go have fun and that he'd catch up with him another time. He knew his twin wouldn't take that as his final answer. Sure enough, thirty seconds later, Joey called him.

Alexander excused himself and then walked down the hall, out of earshot of the group. "What's up JT?"

"Come on, man. You know I've been wanting to check out this new place. I hear the women there are as fine as hell."

"I'm sure they are, but isn't Matteo going with you? I think two Taylor brothers on the prowl is enough for one club. I don't need to tag along."

"If that's the case, forget Matteo. All the ladies really need is me," Joey said. "But seriously, man, we wanted to get you out. Let you see a side of Atlanta you haven't seen in a while." That wasn't the kind of fun Alexander was interested in.

"Nah little brother. Y'all go ahead. You both can tell me all about it tomorrow."

"Alright. But just know you're missing out. Where are you anyway?"

"You're not going to believe it, but I'm at London's place. Her whole family is here. It's like a reunion."

"Are you serious?"

"Yeah. It's already been quite the night with her idiot attorney. The more I think about it, the more I wonder if he's responsible for the attack on the family. It's completely plausible." He filled Joey in on what had just happened. Joey was taken aback. It didn't sound like the same person they had sat across from during the deposition. But then again, he didn't seem like the type to have a two-year affair either.

"I'm going to check out his background. Something's not right with that dude."

"That's a good idea," Alexander replied. "Let me know what you find out."

He was about to end the call when Joey got more serious. "Listen, Alexander, with all of this going on, you should get out of there."

"Why?"

"Do you need a flashing sign? You need to leave that house and everybody in it behind. They're no good for you." Alexander laughed at what he considered to be Joey's overreaction. "I'm serious," Joey said. "Don't stay there long."

"JT, I'm good. We're not at the rehearsal dinner. She already broke up with me. She can't do it again. But don't worry. I won't stay here all night." As those words came out of his mouth, Alexander happened to walk past the guest bedroom. He was caught by surprise, seeing all of his furniture still there. If London didn't want him in her life anymore, why was she holding on to so many of his things?

When Alexander rejoined us, the officers announced that the family was spending the night but recommended the others either leave or spend the night as well. Serena opted to spend the night. Alexander gave me a questioning look.

"I'm fine either way," I said. "You're welcome to stay."

"That settles it then," he replied, smiling.

A moment later, my phone rang. It was Jefferson, suddenly reminding me we weren't there for a family reunion. I put my phone on speaker mode, and Jefferson shared what they had learned from Marge. All I could do was stare at my phone. I couldn't believe I had been the target the whole time.

"Oh, Remy, I'm so sorry you had to endure that and then go away for a month because that woman hated me so much," I said. "We knew she had a problem, but we had no idea it was this bad."

"It's not your fault," Remy replied. "She needs help. But Jefferson, how sure are you that Marge was the head of this and not this Marty as she claimed?"

"We're not a hundred percent sure, but there's no proof yet that someone else was behind any of this. My gut tells me Marge had a partner, but she may have been the ringleader. Let's not forget she killed Wilson."

Luke began pacing. "So, you believe London is the primary target? It's important we're all here tonight, especially if Marge isn't the ringleader. And what does this mean about Kelly's incident?"

She leaned forward, waiting to hear what Jefferson would say. "We're still investigating, but we don't believe Marge was behind it. We think it was . . . coincidental."

"You mean some yahoo ran into her with no connection to the other attacks?" Luke asked.

"That's right," Jefferson replied. "But that's good news in a way. Don't you think, Kelly?"

"I'm glad to hear it may have been some random incident," Kelly replied in relief. "So odd."

I shared what had just taken place with Robert. Jefferson said he would follow up with him in the morning. "That's strange behavior. Alexander, I'm glad you held your own but didn't do anything crazy. I know that must have been a tense few moments for all of you."

"Don't worry. I wasn't going to lose my cool because of him," Alexander said, winking at me. "I wouldn't let my girl see that." Those words slipped so naturally out of his mouth that no one else seemed to pick up on it except Mom, who smiled to herself. She was also studying the exchange between Luke and Kelly. Jefferson's description of Kelly's incident didn't pass the smell test for her.

Poor Kelly, I thought. She was holding onto Luke by a string that was beginning to stretch.

26

"You can do anything but never go against the family."
The Godfather

BEFORE WE CALLED IT A NIGHT, THE OFFICERS SUGGESTED ALEXANDER and Serena move their cars into the garage. They thought having six cars in the driveway and on the street would deter someone from acting out. Normally, that would be a good thing, but the point of the exercise was to see if someone would try to get at me. If someone was out there, the police wanted them to think Luke, Remy, Rod, and I were the only ones in the house.

Since Mom now had the first-floor bedroom, Rod and Remy claimed one upstairs. Serena had her own as well. I was going to sleep in my bedroom, which left one unoccupied room and three remaining guests—Luke, Kelly, and Alexander. That didn't include the officers, who would use the sofa on a rotating duty.

Kelly walked into the last bedroom. "Luke, aren't you coming? Surely you can stand sleeping in the same room with me for one night."

"It's not that. I was just trying to figure out what the best arrangement might be. London, are you just going to leave us hanging?"

I walked out of my bedroom, T-shirt and boy shorts on and toothbrush in hand. "I didn't know you needed room assignments. Kelly, you can sleep in here with me and let the boys fight over the one queen-size bed," I said, smiling. Nobody else thought it was funny. I sighed. "Fine. Luke, sleep with your wife. There are plenty of blankets in the closet if you prefer to sleep on the floor. Xander, you can do the same with me. Is everybody happy now?" They all said yes, as if they needed my approval to claim a spot.

"Kelly, if Luke gets too frisky, just holler, and I'll kick him out for you," Alexander teased as they made their way to the newly assigned bedrooms.

While everyone was upstairs figuring out the sleeping arrangements, unbeknownst to the rest of us, my mom placed a call to Detective Jefferson. "Detective, this is Valentina Devereaux. Sorry for the late call, but I'm a little concerned about a few details you left out earlier. Do you mind clarifying what really happened with Kelly's accident?"

"This is quite a surprise, Mrs. Devereaux. What do you want to know?"

"Please, call me Valentina, and let me get to the point. You indicated it wasn't part of the attacks on my family. So, was it just a coincidence that it was similar to Remy's incident?"

Jefferson hesitated before replying. "I'm not sure I can answer that for you."

"I think you can. In fact, it's the least you can do, Detective. You and your partner have been two steps behind on everything. The family business was attacked, my daughter was almost killed, you faked her death and then sent her away for a month, and now you're telling us London is the real target. Now you're not one hundred percent sure that Marge was heading this all up or if someone else is still out there. Enough with the hemming and hawing. Is Kelly's accident connected or not?"

"Wow. You don't hold back, do you?"

"No, Detective. I do not."

"Alright. In the spirit of moving the investigation forward, I'll tell you what we know. According to the perpetrator, he was paid one thousand dollars to rear-end Kelly and then leave the scene. We can't prove she paid him, although we strongly believe she did, perhaps through a third party. When I told her we knew she paid for the hit, her face turned white. There's surveillance at two ATMs close to her house from the day before. We know she withdrew five hundred dollars on two occasions. Luke was the only person she called after it happened, and she hasn't left his side ever since."

"Do you believe she arranged all of this to get my son's attention?"

"We believe that's the case, but like I said earlier, we're still investigating."

My mother nodded. "Thanks for telling me. My son is very important to me. He will choose who he loves, and I'm fine with that. But I want to make sure he knows the woman he's choosing. If Kelly lied to us to ingratiate herself back into his life, we all need to know, but especially Luke. Don't you think so, Detective?"

"I suppose you're right. I can call Luke first thing in the morning and tell him what we know."

"That's not good enough."

"What do you mean?"

"You need to call Luke now and lay this out for him. He needs to know right now while he's in the same room with her."

"Now?"

"Yes, now!"

Jefferson was still hesitant, but he agreed, thinking Luke might be able to help get at the truth.

"Luke, you don't have to sleep on the floor," Kelly said. "There's no point in you being uncomfortable when you can sleep in the bed. It's not like we haven't slept together before."

Luke was about to answer when he heard his phone ring. He was going to ignore it, but when he saw Jefferson's name on his call display, he picked up. "Hey, Jefferson. What's going on?"

"I know it's late, Luke, but I need to share something with you."

The detective laid most of it out for Luke, including the way Kelly responded at the police station when he confronted her. As Luke listened, he turned away from Kelly. The more he heard, the less he wanted to be in the same room with her, never mind look at her.

"Are you certain about this?"

"As much as we can be, yes. And by the way, your mom knows. She was the one who insisted I call you."

Luke was shaken by the news. Kelly had known their marriage was over, and yet she brought all of them into this, making them believe she was in danger. He came to my room and broke the news to me.

"She has to go," he said when he was finished. "Kelly can't stay in this house tonight. After I talk to her, I'll order an Uber for her to get home. It's not a good idea for me to be near her right now."

"It may be better to have a police officer take her home," I said. "They can take a look around her house to confirm it's safe."

Luke nodded. "I like that idea. I'll talk to Kelly now, then make sure she's ready to leave soon."

"Okay. I'll talk to the officers to see if they can arrange a ride with another officer. I'm sorry Luke. It seems like Kelly is horribly misguided, but don't be too hard on her."

Several minutes later, Kelly walked out of the room carrying her bag and fighting tears. After Luke confronted her, she admitted she had arranged the accident. She wanted to go back to what they had and thought him being concerned about her was the best way to go about it. She said she knew it was a mistake as soon as everyone became so invested in her safety.

"Mistakes are accidents," Luke said. "You made a choice, not a mistake."

She apologized profusely, saying if she could go back in time and undo it, she would, but it was too late. Things were over between them, and there was nothing she could do about it.

Kelly came down the stairs with Luke behind her, stone-faced. She looked like she was doing the "walk of shame," her overnight bag in hand. Remy refused to even look at Kelly. It bothered her that Kelly would stoop so low. How could she try to replicate the attack on Remy? How could she go against the family? We had all bought into her act.

Luke kept his distance while I spoke with Kelly for a few moments. Then I gave her a quick hug, and she was out the door.

27

"When the fox hears the rabbit scream, he comes a runnin' but not to help."

The Silence of the Lambs

MARTY TURNED ONTO LONDON'S STREET JUST AS KELLY WAS LEAVING the house. He pulled over, staying out of sight. He was driving an older black four-door sedan that Marge had arranged for him. Poor Marge. She hadn't stood a chance with the police. Marty had taken special care to ensure there was no connection between her, the goons she had hired, and him. That said, he was surprised to learn she had murdered her boyfriend. Such a shame. He didn't think she had it in her.

Funny, Marty thought, *you just never know people these days.*

Before the police car pulled away, he noticed Luke, Rod,

and Remy were still at the house. Maybe it was time for a change of plans. It was late, which meant they'd all likely go to bed soon. He would take a chance and do something unexpected. He couldn't wait to see their reaction in the morning. That included Kelly. She was never a part of this, but she was so desperate to insert herself back into the family that she deserved a reward for all her efforts. Who was he to deny such a sick, desperate woman? How could they blame him for taking advantage of her poor choices? Knowing where the officer was taking her, he sped up, so he could beat them there.

When they got to Kelly's house, the officer asked Kelly to remain in the kitchen while he checked every room. When he was done, he gave her the all-clear. "No one's here, so you should be fine. After I leave, lock the door and turn the alarm on."

"Thank you. I know I was never really in danger. I'm sorry to have wasted your time."

A few minutes later, the doorbell rang. Thinking the officer had forgotten something, Kelly opened the door without looking through the peephole. "Oh, hi," she said, glancing at her watch. "This is quite a surprise. I don't think you've ever been here before. Come on in."

Marty accepted the invitation. "They must have exiled you just like they do to everyone else."

"Unfortunately, yes. But I deserved it, and I suspect I won't be a Devereaux for much longer. Luke is probably drawing up divorce papers as we speak."

"What is it about that family that makes you want to be around them so badly?" Marty asked as he followed her into the kitchen.

"I don't know," Kelly replied. "I was Luke's wife, but I screwed that up. I gained two sisters, but I messed that up too. I guess I just wanted it all. What about you? What are your thoughts about them?"

"I don't mind telling you the truth, mainly because I know it won't go beyond this conversation."

Kelly thought it was odd that he was willing to open up to her, especially considering she was good friends with London. But whatever. "Of course. It's just between us girls," she kidded.

Marty smiled. "I couldn't care less about that family. They don't mean anything to me. For me it's all about London. I met her years ago, and I was the one she was supposed to be with. But she fell for Alexander. He was wrong, wrong, wrong for her! She's a woman who needs passion and fire, and I can start that fire! That's what I can do for her."

Kelly felt uneasy as he continued.

"But guess what? She figured out on her own she was making a big mistake, and she called off that wedding. Of course, I had no choice but to make sure she saw how much she needed me. And oh, does she need me."

Kelly started putting two and two together. "Wait, are you saying you're behind the arsons and the attack on Remy? All of that just to get London?"

"Well, I can't take all the credit. But yes."

Kelly shook her head. "I don't understand. If you're in love with London, why did you try to destroy her?"

"It's complicated. I thought if I hit the business, she would turn to me. At first, she didn't even notice. I had to start a few fires to get her attention. I turned up the heat, so to say. I lost it for a minute and became enraged when she still ignored me. It really pissed me off, so I arranged for her to be taken. It wasn't supposed to be an accident. That was stupid of me, though. How could I hurt my London? Thankfully, there was a mix-up, and Remy was targeted instead. I took that as another sign from the universe that London and I were meant to be together. I would do anything to have her."

Kelly realized she was staring at a psychopath, and nobody knew it but her. They were only acquaintances, and yet he just admitted he was behind every attack. The fact that he was sharing this with her wasn't good. She knew she had to keep him talking.

"So, what happens next?" she asked, her legs shaking as she walked toward the refrigerator, which was close to the side door. She opened the fridge and then pulled out a bottle of water, setting it on the counter in front of him.

"I drove by London's house just before I came here," Marty said. "I saw Luke, Remy, and Rod were still there. What about the officers? Have they left for the night?"

"Luke, Remy, and Rod were the only ones there when I left," Kelly replied, not wanting to reveal too much information.

"Where was London?"

"I don't know. Now that you mention it, I don't remember seeing her when I left."

His ears perked up. "What do you mean? Where else would she be considering her brother and sister are both there?"

Kelly shrugged. "I'm not sure. I suppose she went out."

Marty took a big sip of water. Then another. She could tell he had lost his composure and was trying to regain it. Just the mention of London going out unnerved him. He was not a stable man. How had he managed to keep it together all this time?

"Thank you, Kelly. You've been helpful. I'll think of you fondly when London and I are together. I know the two of you are good friends. I'll make sure she knows about your help. She'll remember you fondly too—regardless of what the others think about you."

Kelly was sharp enough to know he had just insulted her and more importantly, she had just run out of time.

Running to the side door, she yanked it open and dashed out of the house.

"Help! Help!" she screamed as she ran down her driveway.

Kelly didn't hear it coming, but she felt a sharp, hot pain in her lower back. It hit so hard, it spun her around, and she fell to the ground. She was lying on her side when Marty came and stood over her.

"Sorry, Kelly. I had to shoot you, but don't worry. You

won't die an insignificant death. I'll make sure you go out in a blaze of glory. Literally." She tried to scream again, but no words came out. Marty looked around. All was quiet. Not one good neighbor was there.

Marty carried Kelly back into the kitchen. He laid her on the floor but then thought better of it. She had been helpful; she deserved more than that. He took her to her bedroom and placed her on the bed. He folded her hands, so she looked peaceful, then gave her a kiss on the forehead.

After washing the blood from his hands, he ignited several window treatments, sofas, and clothing with a cigar lighter. Then he slipped away before the fire really got going.

A few blocks away, Marty laid the seat in his car all the way back and closed his eyes. He hadn't believed Kelly when she said London might be out. Considering the circumstances, that was unlikely. She had to be home. Marty had some fun planned for her that night. He wished he could have stayed at Kelly's to see the response to the fire, but that was too dangerous. His priority was London. It always had been. He knew she would be shocked at first, but relief would come at some point when she realized it was him. He had moved well beyond being angry with her and knew it was time for them to be together. There was no need to hurt any other family members unless they got in their way. Regardless of everything that happened, he and London were in love, and everyone would come to understand it. He couldn't wait to be with his dream girl, and he was sure she would feel the same way . . . eventually.

28

"We don't see things as they are, we see things as we are."

Anais Nin

Two hours later, I rolled over and felt a warm, hard body lying next to me. For a second, I didn't know who it was. Then I opened my eyes and saw Alexander spread out on his stomach beneath the covers. I must have stared at him for a full minute, wondering what I should do. He was wearing nothing but gym shorts, and he felt good. I should have known he wasn't going to stay on the rug in front of the bed. It didn't matter how many pillows he had. I couldn't help myself, and I curled up next to him. He smelled good, which made me miss what we had. It was useless when I reminded myself I didn't need him and tried convincing myself I didn't want him. The bottom line was I still loved him. I kissed his wild, curly black hair and then snuck out of bed, smiling to myself. He barely stirred.

I went downstairs, careful to be quiet, knowing I had a full house. On my way into the kitchen for some water, I passed the officers, who were conked out on the two sofas in the family room. So much for protection. I thought about waking one of them but decided to let them sleep. They probably needed it. Plus, if anything happened, they'd be sure to hear it.

I ended up in my office where the lights were off. I looked out the front facing window. We would deal with whatever came our way as a family. But Alexander and I had to figure out where we stood. We hadn't been in the same room in over a year, and yet how we felt about each other was obvious. I needed to remind myself we didn't break up because we fell out of love.

I was lost in thought when I heard someone come up behind me. The room had just enough moonlight to see it was Alexander. We stared at each other, then he came closer and wrapped his arms around me. We stood that way, holding each other in front of the window for several minutes. Then he pulled me away from that vulnerable spot and closed the office doors.

"What are you doing in here?" he asked, holding my hands in his.

"I wanted to get something to drink . . . and to think."

"About?"

"Oh, I don't know. The fact that somebody might be out there waiting in the shadows for me."

"I'm going to put a stop to that," he said as he kissed one of my hands. "What else?"

"Always so confident, aren't you?"

He laughed. "What else were you thinking about?" He kissed my other hand.

"Us and what I should do with you."

"So did you reach any conclusions?"

"Not yet. But I'll let you know when I do," I teased.

"Well, I've been thinking about us for a while—for a year, actually, even more lately. You know you came in rocking that outfit yesterday, don't you?"

"Well, I had to make an impression."

"Oh, you did that. I think you made an impression on every man in the office, including that crazy attorney of yours."

I rolled my eyes. "I don't want to talk about him."

"Neither do I. In fact, amore mio, I don't want to talk about much at all tonight."

He put my hands around his waist. Then he put his hands in my hair and tilted my head back so he could kiss me. It was a real kiss. The intimate kind we hadn't shared for a long time but needed. He still made me feel sexy in a way that no other man did. His hands started moving everywhere, and mine were all over his strong arms and back. As our kiss turned more intense, he picked me up and sat me on the desk. We both wanted this. We couldn't wait anymore. He pulled my shirt over my head, unable to take his eyes off me.

"Get this off," I whispered as I tugged on his shirt. In the few seconds it took for him to remove it, the moonlight caught his eyes. Those eyes . . .

We were skin to skin by then. My heart was already racing as we ravaged each other, but seeing those eyes made my heart beat out of my chest. For a second, I couldn't breathe. His eyes were so familiar, and yet something was missing. They didn't hold the warmth they usually did. They seemed . . . cold. No! It couldn't be!

As my eyes adjusted to the dark, I noticed other things. He had a shirt on, which made sense, but it was a sleeveless hoodie, not the one he had been wearing earlier. He had socks and running shoes on too. Why would he be wearing those?

He started kissing me again, but I turned my head to the side, confused and terrified.

"Alexander?"

"Hmm . . . ?" He replied as he kissed my left ear, my neck, and my shoulder, his hand reaching around behind to unclasp my bra. "Do you remember when I gave you your nickname?"

He slowed a little. "Why don't you remind me?"

The fact that he didn't remember caused my anxiety to spike. Surely Alexander would remember that. "Alexander . . . what's my nickname for you?"

"We'll have plenty of time to talk later," he replied, still focused on my bra.

"Tell me. Right now!"

Finally, he stopped, putting his hands in my hair again. This time he yanked my head back. "I don't know," he said, his voice as cold as his eyes.

"Joey!" I whispered. He opened his mouth to object, but I beat him to it. "Don't try it. I know who you are. Now get the f**k off me. If you kiss me again, I'll bite your f**king tongue off."

Think! Joey told himself. His plan had been to convince London to leave with him as Alexander. He would reveal the truth to her eventually, knowing she would accept him for who he was . . . the man she was meant to be with. But his plan had just run into a hiccup.

"London—"

"Stop. You really need to get off me right now and tell me why you're here! You repulse me, Joey!"

He finally stepped back, which allowed me to run around the desk and put it between us. But now he was blocking my way to the doors. I was shell-shocked and disgusted, but I managed to grab my T-shirt off the floor. I couldn't believe I nearly had some serious "I missed you" sex with Joey Taylor right on Alexander's old desk! I threw up a little in my mouth just thinking about it.

Now that I was away from him, I was more angry than terrified. "Spit it out," I said. "What possible reason do you have for being here in the middle of the night and, worse, for impersonating Alexander? What do you think he's going to say about it?"

"London, I think you knew you were with the wrong twin from the beginning. I was angry about it for a long time, but then you called off the wedding, which was a gift to me. To both of us." He looked me up and down while I put my shirt back on. "He said you were confident. I like that. You're not so lady-like behind closed doors, though, are you?" I wanted to scratch his eyes out. "I did some unorthodox things to let you know it was our time."

"Joey, I don't know what you've been smoking, but you need to stop. Get out!" I yelled. "You should go home, and I'll go back upstairs to your brother. You'll be lucky if I don't press charges against you. You broke into my house and practically assaulted me. Now, I have to shower to get your stench off me!"

Joey froze. "Alexander is still here?"

"Yes. He's been here all night. Come on, let's go." I started to move past the desk but stopped when Joey didn't move. I began to feel uneasy again.

Joey had to calm himself down for the second time tonight. He thought Alexander had left hours ago. Joey had told him to get away from London and her people, not to help Alexander but to help himself. He knew Alexander was still in love with London. Now he was upstairs trying to sleep with her. That was unacceptable.

Joey picked up his gun from a side chair and he made his way around the desk before London could react. "My sweet and spicy London, I'm enjoying our time together. Aren't you?"

He called me the same thing his brother did just a few hours earlier! I didn't respond. I had no idea what he planned to do with that gun, and I didn't want to provoke him.

"Cat got your tongue? Don't worry. We'll be together soon. But you've been getting a little too loud for my comfort. I just need to know who else is here right now. I know Luke, Remy, and Rod are here, so your mother must be here too. Oh, and let's not forget those two officers. They'll be asleep for a while. I took care of that with the help of a bit of hydrogen sulfate, so we wouldn't be disturbed. Is everybody here to protect you from me, London?" He chuckled. "The puzzled look on your face makes me realize you don't know everything I've done for you," he continued. "Now seems like a good time to share."

Beginning with shooting Kelly and setting her house on fire, he worked his way backward from there. I took in every word, tears running down my face. I cried for Kelly, for Wilson, and for Alexander, who would soon learn his twin brother was an arsonist, a traitor, and a murderer.

29

"Don't fight the problem, decide it."
George C. Marshall

"I KNOW IT'S A LOT TO TAKE IN, BUT EVERYTHING I DID WAS OUT OF LOVE for you. I have one task left, then we should get out of here."

"What's that?" I asked.

"I know my brother. His nickname is Pitbull. He'll never accept us being together. He'll work hard to find us and get you back. I need to stop it before it starts."

My pulse began racing again. "What does that mean?"

He smirked. "I think you know."

"Alexander is your twin brother. How could you ever hurt him? It would be like hurting yourself!"

"I chose you over my brother a long time ago."

After everything else he'd said, that didn't surprise me. But it broke my heart, knowing he was willing to kill Alexander because of his twisted fantasy.

He raised the gun. "Listen up, my love. We're going to leave this office. If you yell, scream, or alert anyone in any way, I will go to that bedroom over there," he pointed at it with his gun, "and kill whoever's in there. I suspect it might be your lovely mother. She's such a delight, but I can't let her or anyone else get in our way. Do you understand?"

"I understand. But you need to understand something too. If you do anything to my mother or any other member of my family, you won't live very long. You may not die tonight, but you will die."

Joey took a hard look at me and then laughed. He sounded like Alexander, which irritated me. "I love you, London. I wouldn't expect anything less from you. But don't worry. If you behave, nothing will happen to them."

His eyes darkened, and his face turned serious again. For some reason he paused to look out the window, reflecting for a minute. I was still sitting at the desk and took advantage of his turned back, reaching for my DSIG cell phone in the desk drawer. Knowing the screen would light up, I kept the phone inside the drawer and tried to add a text to the last conversation I had. I wasn't sure who I texted or if the words made sense. At that point, all I could do was send it and pray it went through.

He turned back toward me. For a second, I thought he was on to me. "Let's go. We'll get your mother first. She'll walk upstairs with us."

I held my breath, relieved when he didn't say anything more as I stood up and made my way to him.

He opened the office doors and stopped to tap me on the butt before we walked out. "That's for later," he said. I hadn't cared much for him before, but at that moment my heart blazed with hatred for him.

Joey grabbed my hand and led me to my mother's room.

I wanted to shout out a warning, but I knew better. I thought about the self-defense moves that Remy and I learned in Serena's class. I knew enough to get away from him but not to fight him. But if I got away, where would I go? We were all in my house. He could still shoot me or my mother before anyone else knew what was happening. It wouldn't do any of us any good. We passed the cops, who were still in a deep sleep. True to his word, they were both knocked out and without their weapons.

When we got to Mom's bedroom door, Joey knocked first and asked if she was dressed. He said he was a gentleman and didn't want to embarrass her.

When we entered, Mom sat up, still half asleep. I approached the bed and squeezed her shoulders. "Wake up, Mom. Joey's here. It's been Joey all this time." That woke her up.

"Mama Devereaux, I'm headed upstairs to talk to my brother," Joey said. "You know him well. Do you think he'll understand that London and I are in love?"

Mom blinked a few times, the lights still coming on in her head. "I'm sure he will," she said. "He's a smart man. He's probably seen the signs. But let London tell him while you make plans for the two of you. She broke up with him before, so he's already heard bad news from her. It will come out better that way and maybe even avoid some bad blood between you two."

"That's a good idea, Mom." I forced a smile, then turned to face Joey. "Let me tell him. Then I can meet you at your house, and we can decide where to go from there." It took everything I had to put my hand in his and lead him toward the bedroom door. "I won't be long. I can meet you in thirty minutes."

At first, it seemed like he would go for it, but then he stopped me before I got to the door. "No. That won't work. He'll try to talk you out of being with me. We'll do this my way."

Upstairs, Serena heard her phone buzz for the second time with a text. She had already been tossing and turning, dreaming London was arguing with someone. She reached for her phone and saw it was from London's work number. *Weird,* she thought. There were only five words with no punctuation: "its joey tell alex now" She read it a second time.

"What? Oh crap!" she whispered, then jumped out of bed. So it hadn't been a dream. She must have heard an argument between London and Joey.

Serena grabbed her loaded pistol and opened the bedroom door. Once she confirmed the hallway was clear, she crept to the bedroom where Alexander was sleeping. Serena slipped inside and locked the door behind her. Then she woke Alexander and showed him the text.

"Joey?" he said. "How is that even possible? Surely, she got it wrong. Please God, not Joey." He trusted London with his life, though, and knew she would never send that text if it wasn't true.

He pulled on his clothes, grabbed his Hellcat, and then headed toward the door. "I'm going downstairs to find out what's going on. You know what to do. Call 911, and get everybody up. Tell them to be ready for anything. If Rod is carrying, tell him *not* to shoot my brother!"

"I will. But you need to know: London was downstairs arguing with him. Be careful." He nodded and then went out.

Downstairs, Joey looked at Mom. "Come on, Mommie dearest, you're taking a walk with us. I want both of you upstairs with me." I was trying to stall. I wasn't sure if my text made it or if Alexander was a sitting duck.

"Joey, Mom should stay down here. No need to get her involved in any of this."

Joey didn't buy it. "Both of you, let's move."

We left the bedroom and were making our way toward the staircase when we all stopped short. Alexander was at the bottom of the stairs, staring directly at his twin brother.

"Joey? What's going on? What are you doing here?"

Seeing Alexander caught Joey off guard. Despite all his bravado, he wasn't prepared to talk to his twin.

While the brothers were having a stare-off, I pulled Mom away. We backed out of the family room. Then I ran into her room and grabbed her cell phone. After dialing Detective Jefferson, I handed the phone to her. "Tell Jefferson what's going on while you go next door to the Horns. If they don't answer the door, go to the Banks, then the next house until someone does. But get away from here. I can't risk Joey using you as leverage. One of us will call you once this is over, but I can't lie. This could be ugly. I love you, Mom. Now go!" We hugged, then she raced out the kitchen door.

I could have left with her, but everyone else I loved was still in the house, so I headed back to the family room to see what I could do.

"You're a fool if you think she wants you," Joey said. "She broke up with you because she wanted to be with me. She let you down easy. Time to get over it and move on because that's what London and I are doing."

"And you felt compelled to commit arson and attempt to kill her sister to prove that? JT, you have problems. You need help. You hurt a lot of people because you were obsessed with London. Forget about me. Do you think she'll ever want you after this? What do you think Mama, Gio, and Matteo will say when they find out?"

"As far as I'm concerned there's nothing for them to find out!" Joey replied.

Alexander and Joey were circling each other as if they were about to have an MMA fight. They were wearing different sleeveless hoodies with the same color shorts. Their running shoes were different, but I still had no idea who was who. Because they were identical twins, they made a point of dressing differently at work to preserve their own identities. But outside of the office, things were different. This was not good.

Luke and Rod were on the staircase, ready to pounce but for now they recognized this was brother versus crazy brother, and they didn't intervene. Remy and Serena were likely not too far behind them but out of sight.

"Joey has a gun!" I yelled, looking back and forth as they circled, trying to figure out who was who. They both tensed up.

"Be smart, my Tesoro. Get out of here!" one of them yelled.

"No! Come to me, London."

That was all I needed. Alexander would always try to keep me safe. After noting the color of his shoes, I backed away but stayed close enough to see what would happen next. I didn't have to wait long.

30

"There's no hero without a villain."
Mark Pellegrino

ALEXANDER KNEW HE HAD TO GET LONDON OUT OF JOEY'S WAY. He had lost her once and wasn't going to lose her again. He looked at his twin and saw his own reflection but barely recognized the man Joey had become. He was distraught thinking how his twin brother, the one who had consoled him for months after the breakup, was the person behind this. They had had countless soul-searching conversations about London, about life, and about Alexander moving on in so many ways, and all the while Joey had hid his obsession with her. They knew almost everything about each other, and yet somehow Joey fooled him.

They had both been interested in London when they first met her at a party. Always competitive, they both tried to talk to her, but she blew them off. Other women wanted their attention but not her. London was laughing and talking with some other guy, who seemed intent on making a connection. Alexander was determined too, though.

He knew London's childhood friend, Christian, so he asked her to reintroduce him to London. For him, it was like a backstage pass, and he managed to block the other guy. Every time he moved in, Alexander stepped in front of him. The dude didn't have a chance, and neither did Joey. They talked for hours, and that very night, London made her choice.

Joey had talked smack about Alexander not being good enough for a woman like that, but looking back now, Alexander realized Joey was jealous. The women he dated after that party all resembled London, but they were never the total package, only able to hold their own until Joey got bored. Now Alexander knew why there were so many. All of them were missing one thing. They weren't London.

His Hellcat was tucked inside his shorts. His plan was to keep Joey talking until the police came. Then there would be no need to use it. He knew if he pulled it out, he had to be willing to pull the trigger. London had warned him about Joey's gun, but surely, Joey wouldn't threaten him with it.

"So, what's the plan lil' bro?" Alexander asked. "You're going to leave here and then what? You want to live happily ever after with my girl? Is that it?"

"She's not your girl," Joey replied.

"Well, she damn sure isn't yours. The best thing you can do is let the police take you into custody when they get here. There's no point in dragging this out. You have a lot to make amends for already."

Joey had planned to take Alexander by surprise. He hadn't thought about the police. Other than Kelly, London was the only other person he had confessed to. But Alexander had been ready for him and knew he was behind what happened to the Devereauxs. Things started to click in Joey's mind. He glanced at London and then back at this brother. "How did you get a heads-up? After she came down here, she was with me the whole time. I watched her walk down the stairs alone, go into the kitchen, and then the office. That's where we spent our time together tonight." He unleashed a malicious smile. "By the way, you never told me she was such a good kisser and I suspect so much more. Making out with London on your desk gave me a nice preview. I can't wait for the full show."

It was a good thing I didn't have a gun, or I might have shot Joey on the spot. The look on Alexander's face said he was getting close to doing it himself.

"And, bro the feel of those ti—"

"Stop it! Just stop it!" I yelled. You attempted to destroy me and my family because you love me? Then you killed Kelly, who had nothing to do with any of this, and now you think I'm running away with you? That will never happen! I don't love you. I loathe you!"

No one else had known about Kelly until that moment. Everybody was silent for a few seconds. Then chaos ensued.

Luke and Rod rushed down the stairs, Remy and Serena right behind them. Luke jumped into Joey's face. "You killed Kelly?"

He chuckled. "Yes! One of you had to die!"

"No! It can't be!" Remy screamed. "You sick, pathetic excuse for a man. You'll pay for this! I swear you'll pay!"

I had already cried for Kelly, and I knew I would again, but it was heartbreaking to see Luke and Remy's reaction. I knew my siblings were thinking of how things had ended with Kelly a few hours earlier, but there was no way we could have known.

Luke punched Joey in the face. He got in a few more shots before Rod and Alexander pulled him off. He was so enraged that the two of them could barely hold him back. I would have let Luke beat him up a little longer.

Unprepared for the blows, Joey lost his footing, but he leaped right back up. His right eye showed signs of swelling right away. Then I saw the look in his eyes. Always the eyes . . . Then everything unfolded like a movie in slow motion.

Realizing he was outnumbered, Joey pulled the gun from under his shirt. He aimed it at Luke, then pointed it at Remy, whose screams had turned to tears, and then at Alexander, as if unsure who he should kill first.

"Gun!" Alexander shouted. He covered Luke while pulling out his weapon and aiming it at Joey. At the same time, Rod pulled Remy and Serena back to the hidden part of the staircase. I turned to run into the kitchen when someone grabbed the back of my T-shirt. Joey pulled me close and held me in front of him, his gun pointed at Alexander.

"London, I'm afraid we can't stay much longer," Joey said, into my ear, his eyes fixed on his brother. "I'm going to need you to drive. I don't want you to get hurt, but you should know, I'm not afraid to die because I know you'll be right there with me."

I started shaking. What was he saying?

"JT," Alexander said, his voice calm as he tried to deescalate the situation. "Do you think holding a gun right on London is going to entice her to go anywhere with you?"

"Well, if you put your gun down, I'll put mine down," Joey replied.

Alexander shook his head. "Not gonna happen. You have to let London go first."

As the brothers went back and forth, I heard police sirens approaching. I just hoped they arrived before any of us got hurt.

Joey's hold on me loosened as he and Alexander continued to exchange jabs. I tried again to remember the defensive moves I knew. I recalled I was supposed to use my elbows, knees, and head rather than my fists.

Joey was still distracted and already injured from Luke's attack, so I elbowed him in the stomach. It caught him by surprise, which was the point. I turned around and grabbed his hair, pulling his head down as I smashed my knee into his nose. His nose didn't break, but it was enough to cause him to release his hold on me. But before I could get away, he grabbed me again. He was desperate.

"Joey let her go. Don't make me shoot you!" Alexander pleaded. I could tell he was torn up inside. I knew it wasn't my fault, but I wished I was strong enough to get away. I didn't want to force that choice on him.

When he raised his gun, he had tears in his eyes. It was as if Joey had a death wish because he raised his gun as well. In the second it took for the brothers to pull the trigger, Serena appeared on the staircase and fired two shots. Both of them hit Joey in the right shoulder.

Joey's body spun, sending me flying backward. My head hit the stone coffee table, then I landed on the floor. Joey was also on the floor, writhing in pain.

Before I realized it, Alexander was next to me. "Amore mio," he said, kissing me. I kissed him back, only to realize he was bleeding. Why was he bleeding? Then it registered. Joey had gotten off a shot before he went down. Had he hit Alexander?

No! my mind screamed. Then everything went black.

31

"There is only one difference between a madman and me. The madman thinks he is sane. I know I am mad."

Salvador Dali

LUKE, REMY, ROD, AND I WATCHED THE POLICE DEPARTMENT'S PRESS conference on TV in my hospital room. The original intent was for my family and me to join them to announce that Remy was alive, but instead, it turned into an announcement that everyone was safe from a madman. Jefferson took the lead. "Joseph Flavio Taylor, a prominent attorney in the Atlanta area, was apprehended at approximately three o'clock this morning. We are confident he was the criminal mastermind behind several arsons throughout the Atlanta metro area, one murder, an attempted murder, and an attempted kidnapping targeting the Devereaux family and their business, Devereaux and Sinclair Insurance Group. More charges are being considered in Georgia and Louisiana.

"Mr. Taylor is the twin brother and business partner of Attorney Alexander Tommaso Taylor, who was at one time engaged to London Devereaux. We believe Ms. Devereaux was the primary target of the assaults. Her sister and business partner, Remy Devereaux, was run off the road and presumed dead several weeks ago. However, today we are also here to announce that Remy Devereaux is alive after the failed attempt on her life formulated by Joseph Taylor."

Several reporters had questions. "Detective, how was Joseph Taylor apprehended?"

"Mr. Taylor held most of the Devereaux family, his brother, and one other person hostage at London Devereaux's home. The family matriarch, Valentina Devereaux was able to escape and call 911. The police surrounded the house and entered the premises, whereupon we arrested the subject."

"Was Joseph Taylor or anyone else injured in the process?" another report asked. "I understand that at least two ambulances arrived at the home. Is it true that several people were injured before you arrived?"

Before Jefferson could respond, more questions came. "If so, how serious are the injuries, and who was hurt? Weren't there police officers in the house who could have prevented this?"

"It's true that three people were wounded before our arrival," Jefferson said. "None of those injuries are life-threatening. I won't reveal the names due to privacy issues."

"And what about the officers inside?"

"I have no comment at this time about any officers in the home."

I knew it was embarrassing for the police to admit the two officers had been outsmarted and overcome by Joey, hence Jefferson's avoidance of the question.

Luke turned off the TV. It was our story. We didn't need to hear it from the detectives' perspective. We were still processing everything. Even though Joey wasn't my favorite person, I would have never thought he was capable of this. It would take time for us to recover from the deaths of Kelly and Wilson as well as Alexander's shooting. It was all so surreal.

Right as Serena shot Joey, he shot Alexander. They were both hit in the right shoulder. The universe was determined to keep them connected even if they didn't want to be. They were both recovering from surgery and would make a full recovery. The difference was that Joey would be handcuffed to his hospital bed.

As for me, I would also recover—at least physically. I suffered a concussion from hitting the table and needed a few stitches in the back of my head. I was still surprised that Joey had pushed me out of the way when the gunfire started. In his irrational way, he believed we were meant to be together and didn't want me to get hurt. I'll never understand it.

While I was musing over that, Mom entered the room. She had left earlier to check on Alexander. She still felt responsible for Kelly's death, but Luke told her there was no way any of us could have known what Joey had planned. If we did, we would have tried to keep her safe. But there was no way we could keep her safe from a madman.

"Alexander is awake now," Mom said. "He's asking to see you, London. I told him you'll be released soon and will check on him then. Joey hasn't come out of recovery yet."

"Thanks, Mom." I was going to ask Luke to hand me the phone but then thought better of it. He was somber, standing with his arms crossed. He was hurting more than the rest of us.

"Luke, I don't know how we'll move past this, especially what happened to Kelly," I said. "It doesn't matter that you were separated. She was still your wife and my friend. We'll figure this out together one day at a time, okay?" He nodded. Remy and Mom gave him a hug. I would have joined in if I could.

I called Alexander's room, and his mother answered the phone. She had been in the US for over forty years and had spent much of that time married to her African American husband and the father of her four sons. I hadn't spoken to her in a long time. "Hi, Mama Lucia. It's London."

"London, mia figlia!" she said in her Italian accent. Alexander had taught me enough Italian to know that "mia figlia" meant "my daughter." I was happy she still felt that way. She must have been torn up inside. The idea of having one of her sons turn against his twin was heart-wrenching. I wondered if she blamed me for Joey's obsession, but her response let me know that wasn't the case. She told me Alexander was still a little groggy but to come see them as soon as I could.

As I hung up with Mrs. Taylor, Serena entered the room.

"Serena!" I said. "You're our hero! How in the world were you able to pull that off?" It was the first time I'd seen her since the incident.

Serena's face was stoic. She had come to my house because she was mourning Wilson's death. She had no idea the night would end with her shooting someone. "I usually keep a pistol hidden in an ankle holster when I'm off duty. When I got your text, I was ready just in case. And I'm glad I was."

"We're all glad you were!" Luke said. "You saved our lives."

Mom teared up as she gripped Serena's arm. "Thank you."

The doctor came in shortly after that and cleared me to go home. Once I was ready to leave, we went to see Alexander. Matteo, Gio, his wife, Cali, and their mother, Lucia were there. Alexander was sitting up in bed with a sling on his left arm. As soon as he saw me, his face burst into a smile.

I don't know who hugs more, my Southern family or his Italian family, but it was a full-blown hug fest.

"Hey, can I get in on some of that?" Alexander asked. Careful not to hurt his shoulder, I hugged him as best as I could, then gave him a kiss. "I missed you," he said, then kissed me back. All eyes were on us in that small room, so we both pulled back. We would have plenty of time later to decide our future.

"Excuse me, Alexander and Lucia Taylor?" a doctor asked as he entered the room. "You're both listed as Joseph Taylor's next of kin. I need to talk to you about his recovery."

"You can share whatever news you have in front of everyone," Mama Lucia said.

"Alright. Well, there's been a complication. Joey came out of surgery and will make a full recovery. However, he's had some memory loss."

"What does that mean?" Alexander asked.

"He can't remember anything. He doesn't know what happened, and he doesn't know who he is. He has amnesia."

None of us believed that for one minute. Joey was an astute attorney. He was probably plotting how to delay or avoid a trial, not to mention prison time.

"I need to talk to him. Right now!" Alexander said. The doctor tried to object, but even with only one arm working fully, Alexander was formidable.

"Mama and I will go talk to him," Gio said. "You stay put, lil' brother."

"No. I'll go, and London too."

"Me?" I asked. "Why would you want me to see him?"

"I know my brother. In his sick mind, this was all about you. If he's faking amnesia, it will be difficult to pretend he doesn't know you."

Nobody was happy about it, but he was right. So, overruling everyone's objections, Alexander and I headed to Joey's room.

When we walked in, Joey appeared to be sleeping, but he opened his eyes when he heard us approach. It still amazed me how he was the mirror image of his brother. He studied us for a few seconds before speaking. "You look just like me. You must be the twin I was told about. And you . . . " He looked me up and down. "You must be London. You're even more beautiful than I imagined. Why would I try to hurt you? I can't believe I did any of what I've been told I did to you and so many others. If it's true, it's horrible, and I can't apologize enough."

"What's the last thing you remember?" I asked.

"I don't have any memories. I woke up in this hospital and was told why I had surgery, and I've been trying to put the pieces together ever since."

"I call BS on that," Alexander said angrily. "I know this is some sort of scheme, but it won't work, Joey. You've been charged with murder and more. You did it all, and you even tried to kill me, your twin brother! Even if you don't remember it, we do."

"Maybe it's better that I don't remember," Joey said. "I don't want to be the monster they described. I can't imagine doing any of those things. Both of you . . . please forgive me."

As I stared at Joey, I couldn't tell if he was being sincere or not. His eyes weren't cold; they were desperate, as if he had just realized the consequences he was facing.

"It's too late," I said. "I don't want your apology."

Alexander and I left, determined that Joey would face justice for everything he had done. Although I knew Joey would always be a part of our lives, from the moment I walked out of that hospital room, he was dead to me.

EPILOGUE

"And I'd choose you; in a hundred lifetimes, in a hundred worlds, in any version of reality, I'd find you and I'd choose you."
The Chaos of Stars

SIX MONTHS LATER . . . CHRISTMAS

Rod was moving from station to station, checking the food quality in the expansive kitchen. The absolute best was expected from everyone. He was excited and stressed at the same time. He and Remy were finally living their dream. Their restaurant, the Sophia, was having its soft opening, and they both wanted everything to go perfectly. If the restaurant was successful, they planned to open a second more casual restaurant called Sophia and Leo's Kitchen. That night, only family, close friends, and a few strategic guests were invited.

Rod left the kitchen and found Remy in the private dining room. She looked stunning as she greeted guests in her shimmering gold gown. It made her green eyes shine even brighter than normal.

The room was decorated in white, silver, and gold for the holidays. Several Christmas wreaths and trees of varying sizes filled the space. The largest tree, located in the center of the restaurant, was twenty feet tall. It was beautiful and majestic, but his favorite tree was by the hostess station. It was a Creole Christmas tree topped with Papa Noel. He and Remy had a similar one in their home.

The invitations had suggested holiday attire, and the guests didn't disappoint. There were lots of black, red, and silver dresses, and most of the men were in suits or tuxedos. Rod wore a traditional black tuxedo with a red pocket square.

As drinks and hors d'oeuvres flowed, Rod made his way through the gathering. "Ladies, you look beautiful tonight," he said to Remy and his mother-in-law, who was wearing a beaded red dress. He gave Remy a kiss.

"Thank you, and you look quite handsome in your tuxedo," Remy's mother said.

"Thanks, Mom. I can clean up when I have to." He smiled, then looked at Remy. "Dinner is in thirty minutes. Your people better not be late!"

"They'll be here," Remy assured him. "You know Luke is bringing his lady friend tonight. We finally get to meet Madison."

"I'm looking forward to it. Well, more guests are arriving, so I'll make the rounds."

"Are you sure Luke is okay?" Mom asked when he left. "I've been worried about him."

"I think so," Remy replied. "I'm just glad he's back at work and seeing Madison again. I think he'll be fine eventually, but Kelly will remain in his heart." Mom nodded in agreement. "Speaking of Luke, there he is now. And there's Madison!"

Remy and Mom tried not to be obvious as they checked

out the woman who had Luke's attention.

Across the room, Madison leaned in close to Luke. "I'm a little nervous to meet your family tonight."

He smiled. "Trust me, you're good. Everybody's looking forward to you being here. Plus, the spotlight won't be on us."

He didn't elaborate as Mom and Remy made a beeline toward them. After making the introductions, Luke downplayed the importance of Madison meeting the family. He had no doubt he'd hear their opinions the following day. Madison was Asian with long, dark, wavy hair. She was petite, no more than five feet two inches without her heels and had a surprisingly deep tan. She seemed confident, and Remy liked her right away, though she had to remind herself not to compare Madison to Kelly.

"Where's London?" Luke asked.

"She's not here yet," Remy said. "I'm going to text her. She needs to get here before we move to the tables for dinner. It's almost time." After sending a text, she got a swift reply. "She said she'll be here before seven and to have a glass of Veuve to calm my nerves! Typical London."

I knew we were running late, but we were almost there. Alexander was driving while I texted Remy.

"I was thinking Alexandria might be a good name for a girl," he said out of the blue.

I looked at him in surprise. "Alexandria? A good name for whose girl?"

He glanced at me and then turned his attention back to the road. "Or maybe Alex could be a good name for a son."

I was still perplexed. "Whose children do you want to be named after you? Is Cali pregnant again, and you're trying to convince Gio to name their baby after you?"

"That would be funny, but no. I'm talking about us. You know, if we started a family."

"But, Xander, you don't want any children, remember?"

When we pulled up to the Sophia, Alexander gave my left hand a quick squeeze as the valet opened my car door. By the time I got out and adjusted my figure-fitting winter-white gown, Alexander was by my side. He looked so handsome in his white tuxedo jacket. The black skinny tie and black pocket square looked perfect with it.

The restaurant's double doors had a large wreath with white lights hanging over them. Two greeters opened the doors for us. Alexander faced me and took my hands in his. "But what if I did? What if I wanted children? Would you want a few little A's running around?"

I couldn't help but laugh at the thought of little A's. "I'll have to think about that. But maybe." I smiled. Then he kissed me hard. "I love you, Xander," I said.

"I love you more, so much more," he replied. Then, arm in arm, we made our grand entrance into the restaurant.

Mom and Mama Lucia were the first people we saw. "Look at you two," I said. "If I didn't know any better, I'd think you're looking for some action tonight! They both laughed.

"Well, you never know. The night is young," Mom joked.

Alexander hugged them both. His mother kissed him on both cheeks, then asked him something in Italian. He winked and nodded at her. I saw Remy and excused myself.

"Sissy, I can't believe how gorgeous everything looks!" She and I had spent hours planning where every tree, wreath, light, and garland would go. It was perfect.

"I know, right?" she said. "I mean, thank you! Listen, before everyone sits down, I want you to see someone who begged to come."

"Who?" I asked, and then I saw him as he made his way toward us with his slicked-down red hair. "Robert, it's been a while."

"I missed you, London," he replied. "When I heard about the Sophia, I asked Remy for an invite. I wanted to see you both. I hope we can put everything behind us." He was about to go on when I interrupted him.

"No need to continue, Robert. At least you were in the ballpark. It was a Taylor brother, just not the right one. The rest is almost history."

"Yes, I did get that wrong, and I'm glad for that. Under the circumstances, it looks like things turned out as best as they could." His wife, Amy, joined us. "You remember Amy, don't you?"

"Of course! Amy, it's good to see you again," I said, and I meant it. We exchanged quick hugs.

Alexander walked up and hugged me from behind, having overheard the tail end of our conversation. "Oh, I think some things turned out for the best. But not everything." He kissed my neck.

"Sorry to break this up," Remy said, "but it's time to move into the main dining room for dinner."

Before Robert went to his table, we agreed to talk later. I noticed he and Alexander didn't shake hands.

"I still don't like him," Alexander said. "There's more to the story than you know."

"I don't blame you, my love, and you can fill me in later," I replied. Then I grabbed two glasses of champagne from a passing server and gave him one. "To the Sophia," I said, raising my glass. He smiled and clinked glasses with me.

"And to us."

As everyone migrated into the main dining room, which was dominated by the huge Christmas tree, I felt good. It was mid-December, my favorite time of year. Despite all that had happened over the past six months, life was feeling more normal each day.

When we reached our table, I was floored to see my two best friends, Christian and Suzette. I had no idea they would be there. "Why didn't anybody tell me you were coming?" I asked. "This is such a surprise!" They didn't live in Atlanta, and I hadn't seen them since before the Joey incident, although they knew all about it. After we hugged, they were seated at the table next to us, so we'd have to talk later. *How exciting,* I thought. I hadn't seen my besties in a long time.

Our table was round and set for ten. It was beautiful. Charcuterie boards, specialty bread baskets, wine, and more cold champagne were waiting for us. Remy, Rod, Luke, Madison, Mom, Mama Lucia, Serena, and her friend, whom we just met, were all sitting at the table with us. I had met Madison by accident when she was leaving Luke's place early one morning, which is another story, but I liked her. We agreed that she, Serena, Remy, and I would have a girls' night out. Ever since Serena saved our lives that night, she had become a part of the family. She would never be lonely for company again.

About sixty people were seated, and I knew most of them. Rod and Remy stood up to thank everyone for coming. They also shared about how they didn't think the restaurant would happen, and yet there we all were. Rod thanked Remy for her love, persistence, and hard work. It was quite touching. I was thrilled for them. They had finally followed their dream, and I knew the Sophia would be a success.

"Although we're happy to celebrate our soft opening with all of you, that's not the only reason we're celebrating tonight," Rod said. Then he came over and handed the mic to Alexander, who stood up and shook his hand.

"Xander, what in the world are you doing?" I whispered. I heard a few chuckles from our table but was too fixated on Alexander to determine who it was. He looked nervous. He held out his hand and gave me a devilish smile. I took it and stood up. Then he stepped back so he could look into my eyes as he spoke. As soon as he opened his mouth, the restaurant and everyone in it disappeared. I could hear and see only him.

"London, amore mio, I was drawn to you the moment I saw you three years ago, but it wasn't until after we met that I realized I was missing something huge in my life. With you, I felt whole for the first time. When we didn't see each other, we made a point to talk. If we couldn't talk, we would text, and during those few times we couldn't text, I thought about you and hoped you were thinking about me too.

"You made me the happiest man alive when you said yes two years ago. But the truth is, as much as we loved each other, we weren't ready. I was devastated when you called off the wedding, but I knew it wasn't the end of us. We needed to experience life apart to enjoy the rest of it together. No matter how far apart we were over the past year, I knew I'd choose you over and over again."

Alexander released my hand. Then he pulled out a small box and got down on one knee. To my surprise, the box contained a different engagement ring that shone even brighter than the one I had returned to him. "London Devereaux, would you do me the honor of becoming my wife, my partner, my lover, and the mother of my future children, for real this time?"

I had not expected it that night, but as the room came back into focus, I saw that my family had. They knew. As I looked at the smiling faces at my table, I realized that Mom, Mama Lucia, Luke, Remy, and Rod all knew! I looked at the next table and saw my besties, Christian and Suzette. They knew too. That's why they were there. It all made sense. The tragedy and the ugliness that we experienced had brought us all closer. We were a family, and Alexander was a part of that family. It could no longer be denied.

"Yes!" I said, "I'll marry you. You're the only one I belong to. I don't want to spend another day without you in my life."

He placed the ring on my finger then jumped up. "She said yes!" Everybody leaped to their feet, clapping and cheering as we kissed.

The rest of the night was perfect. Rod, Remy, and Alexander spared no expense. The Sophia's soft opening, which I had helped plan, turned out to be my surprise engagement party. We celebrated with family and friends for hours, then Alexander and I were the first to leave. For the first time in a long while, all was well with the world because we had chosen each other for real this time.

"The judge agreed with the prosecution," Joey's lawyer told him. "They denied our motion, which claimed you couldn't be tried if you can't assist in your own defense."

Joey was livid. A severe case of amnesia should have been enough to delay the trial. But that wasn't how the judge saw it. "I had a feeling the judge wouldn't be empathic toward me," he said. "I've won more cases in his courtroom than I can remember, and that's despite some of his rulings against my clients. He hardly ever ruled in my favor."

"How do you know that?" his lawyer asked, giving him a curious look. "You don't recall anything from your past since you were shot six months ago."

Joey shrugged. "That was plan A. It's kept me out of that disgusting county jail all this time. Although there are plenty of looney toons here, this medical facility is much better. But don't worry. If you've learned anything about me, you should know I'm resilient."

His attorney was concerned by this revelation, but before he could say anymore, his cell phone rang. It was an unknown caller. He was going to ignore the call, but Joey gestured for him to answer it.

"Hello?" He paused to listen. "How did you get this number? Yes. I'm with him now, but—" He listened for a moment and then handed the phone to Joey. "It's for you."

Joey took the phone. "Yes?" As he listened, he became agitated. "He did that tonight in front of everyone? He's an idiot! It's only been six months." He listened again, nodding. "You did the right thing by calling. I appreciate the partnership. You know, I couldn't have done all of this without you, Robert."

"There's no partnership. You're blackmailing me!"

"Two things can be true at once," Joey said. "But I'm not the one who had a two-year affair." Then he disconnected the call. He looked at his attorney with a familiar coldness in his eyes and a new determination on his face. "My brother just forced my hand. It's time to implement plan B."

ACKNOWLEDGEMENTS

A HUGE THANK YOU TO MY MOTHER AND SISSY, WHOM I HARASSED throughout this entire process. You read every line repeatedly without complaining even though I know you wanted to. Sissy, if it wasn't for your wild imagination, the Devereauxs might not exist. We had no idea who they would become.

Thank you to Michel, Patrice, and Sandi for being beta readers and providing your feedback at varying stages. It made a huge difference. Jadah, and Sara, your input was more helpful than you'll ever know.

To my editor and book cover designer, I feel like I walked out of the salon with a fresh blowout and makeup. You sure know how to clean a book up!

Rod, I made one call, and you jumped into action when I was overwhelmed. Thank you for guiding me. I don't know if I'll ever be able to repay your kindness.

Terrell, thank you for being my "30"! Even though you refused to read it until I was done with the first draft, your gasp when you learned Marty's identity said it all! Thank you for putting up with my writing on champagne Sundays, late nights, and much more. I love you, lover.

Made in the USA
Columbia, SC
26 April 2024